FOUR IN THE MORNING

FOUR IN THE MORNING

ESSAYS BY SY SAFRANSKY

Published by

THE SUN PUBLISHING COMPANY

Chapel Hill, North Carolina

Manufactured in the United States of America

Published by
The Sun Publishing Company
107 North Roberson Street
Chapel Hill, North Carolina 27516
919 942–5282

Ordering information:
To order additional copies directly from the publisher, send $13.95 (paperback) or $19.95 (hardcover) plus $2 postage and handling for each book to The Sun Publishing Company, 107 North Roberson Street, Chapel Hill, NC 27516

Library of Congress Cataloging-in-Publication Data
Safransky, Sy
Four in the morning: essays by Sy Safransky
814.54 93-83779

ISBN 1-883235-13-8 (paperback)
     1-883235-12-X (hardcover)

FOR NORMA

CONTENTS

PREFACE

Selecting my favorite essays has been like trying to herd thirty rowdy kids onto a bus. They were written to stand on their own, they insisted. Each was unique, each deserved a window seat. Then, too, just about all of them showed up with extra luggage that needed to be left behind. That's when they discovered they weren't so unique: certain themes repeated themselves, a few images had slept around.

Read them as you would a sheaf of letters from a friend, making allowances for the coffee stains and loopy handwriting and words crowded together at the end of the page: it's been a bumpy ride. Careful editing has made the pieces slightly more readable, but I didn't want to be too careful; written over a period of nearly ten years, the essays reflect different answers to questions that themselves keep changing.

For giving *Four In The Morning* such an elegant look, thanks to designer Sue Koenigshofer. For help with editing, I'm grateful to my wife Norma as well as Dana Branscum, Terry Toma, Jan Bellard, Pamela Penick, Jeff Qualls, and Cassandra Sitterly. Valuable suggestions also came from Elizabeth Rose Campbell, Carol Logie, Sam Gaines, Cindy Calderwood, and Diana Hall. With so many cooks bent over one stewpot, you'd think I could blame someone else for any mistakes, but responsibility is mine.

Sy Safransky

BITTER MEDICINE

THE GREAT TEACHER Marpa was grieving. His oldest son had been killed. One of Marpa's students came to him and said, "I don't understand. You teach that all is an illusion. Yet you are crying. If all is an illusion, then why do you grieve so deeply?" Marpa replied, "Indeed, everything is an illusion. And the death of a child is the greatest of these illusions."

If my son, Joshua, had lived, he'd be a teenager now. But I don't know what that means. It's a thought with dark wings that drag the ground. I push it off the edge of my mind and it falls and falls, turning like the seasons, smashing against the rocks below.

Born prematurely, Joshua was kept alive for three days. I'm not sure how much he suffered, or why he was born too soon or died too soon; these thoughts, too, fall into the mind's abyss, screeching their *if onlys*.

A hundred years ago, Joshua would have died between his mother's legs. A decade ago, machines kept him warm, breathed for him, extended for a while his life, our life together. I wanted him to live, desperately. I wanted bigger machines, technological miracles. I wanted the Industrial Revolution by my side as I chased death down the hospital halls and out the big glass doors. I wanted the doctors wakened from sleep to rush to his side, and pull from their little black bags every trick.

My brother-in-law wrote out the Sanskrit symbol for "Om" and taped it to Joshua's incubator. I was moved by the gesture, though I didn't really understand. I'd only recently begun the slow drift away from conventional views into the roiling blackness and uncertainty I called spirituality, a darkening whirlpool taking me down. My old life was breaking up, drifting, dying, and my son's birth and struggle for life was a storm that broke yet more of me, wave upon wave of pain like cold rain. To keep him from dying, I would have done anything; had someone with a knowing look told me to sacrifice the neighbor's cat, I would have been out at midnight with a knife between my teeth.

The truth is, I couldn't even pay the bill. It cost more to keep Joshua alive those few days than to feed countless hungry children for countless days. I didn't care. It was futile, we all knew it. But the doctors didn't care. I mean, they did care. I mean, I don't know. Here was Medicine, down in the dirt with Death, fighting for my son's life. Here was an act of love, wasn't it? Here was sacrifice, but whose? Here was faith, but in what?

I was sure of one thing: this was the greatest pain I'd ever known. My fortress mind was taken completely by surprise. I used to hide when life knocked with its big fist on the door — up high, inside the turrets, taking aim with words. Words were useless now. And so my life seemed useless. The pain was more real to me than my writing, my marriage, my future. My life had been full of possibility — choices that spiraled dizzily into clouds, ambition's endless horizon. And this was the end of the world. Not really — I ate, slept, slept some more. I continued. But something had died in me. I'd reached into my own little black bag, and for the first time had come up empty-handed.

Two years later, in another hospital five hundred miles away, my father lay dying of cancer.

In the beginning, he thought the pain was from intestinal gas. "Why can't they do something for the gas?" he asked. It wasn't gas; it was the tumor, advancing on his liver. The doctors assured him they were doing all they could — except telling him the truth, which he finally figured out for himself.

I tried. Stop eating foods with preservatives, cut down on meat, I told him, while he sipped a Pink Grapefruit No-Cal, unimpressed. Turn off the television, I said. Reluctantly, he lowered the sound. Every few months, I swept into his life like an airplane dropping leaflets. Surrender or die, they said. Go to hell, said he.

What was he supposed to do? Give up his life so he could live? To change his ways seemed to him like just such a sacrifice; it must have seemed that way to the doctors, too, who never even suggested it.

It was early morning, when hospitals are most like monasteries. A bell chimed softly. In the dimly lit hall, ghostly figures made their rounds, intent on salvation, of bodies if not souls, passing by my father's room where a real ghost hovered, unsure whether to return to its condemned house, the windows broken, rotting timbers showing, the body a slum now loved by no one, once proud, now pissed on and ruined, like the old city he loved, Broadway with its lights and high buildings reaching higher. What the politicians had done for New York the doctors had done for him.

When my mother and I arrived, he seemed asleep, his eyes half-open, face bathed in sunlight. I hadn't seen him this relaxed. "Mom," I said, reaching for her. "I don't think he's breathing." She took my hand. For a moment, we stood motionless, awed by the mystery of his lifeless body. Then she called for a doctor, who told us to wait outside. We did, as another doctor arrived, and another. It was ten minutes before one of them spoke to us. They'd done all they could, the doctor said.

The occasion for these reminiscences? This fall, my wife will enter medical school. As a college freshman, ten years ago, she decided she wanted to be a doctor. When she graduated, she got married instead. She had a son and five years later got divorced. The boy's father moved away and she lost a court fight to keep the child. Saddened, seasoned, she gets her chance again; I get a chance, too — to get out of the way.

It hasn't been easy. I have my reasons for not wanting her to go, and I have my other reasons, fears curled within fears, dark flowers that bloom at night, the past's thorny kiss.

This is my third marriage. I want it to last. And medical school doesn't leave much time for marriage, or anything else. It's an initiation into a priesthood, meant to separate the elect from the rest of us, so the higher mysteries remain mysterious, so doctors can keep fooling not just us, but themselves.

I don't like the profession. It reduces the body, like a machine, to its parts, instead of dealing with the whole person, the passions, the spirit that moves us. Its emphasis on the so-called building blocks of life, on the intricacies and behavior of cells, is intellectually stirring but misses too much; it's like trying to understand the heart of a great city by studying its traffic patterns. How strange, too, that medicine, which brings its big guns down on little germs the way the United States trounces on Grenada, which rolls its depth charges into the murky seas of us, cuts and slashes through the jungles of us, lies down with death and even in dreams lays ambush for death, how strange that medicine so denies death, tries to cheat it by doing everything possible to delay it, for years, months, hours, for ridiculous minutes, cheating us of a good death, not to mention a good life, magnifying our fears instead of helping us face them. And then, with Olympian arrogance, boasting that medical advances are responsible for our longer lives, ignoring the combined effects of better nutrition, cleaner water, sewage treatment, and more, much more. This is like your car mechanic boasting because you've bought a new car. I could go on.

And I have, many times — about not wanting my wife gone for ten, twelve, fourteen, God-knows-how-many hours a day, married not to me but to her work, in a man's world where I don't speak the language and don't want to — my voice cutting the night like an ambulance siren, racing through my mind's back streets, picking up speed, taking shortcuts . . . but who am I trying to save?

Myself? Haven't I learned better by now? Our marriage? On the contrary. The more I try to nudge Norma off her chosen path, the more I push our marriage toward oblivion. I've been going about this the way doctors try to treat an illness, interfering with a process they think they understand; imagining they know what's best; avoiding, at all costs, suffering.

The irony is that I'm really not against her being a doctor. My intuition says she'll be good, the exception to the rule: independent, challenging the conventional wisdom, motivated not by the desire for wealth or status but the yearning to help.

No, the truth is simpler: I fear being left alone. I fear living without a woman's constant companionship, approval, affection, depending on her like a pill taken at regular intervals, like visits to the doctor.

That's the crux of it: my fear, not her career. My buried pain, its ghoulish hand rising up at night to seize me by the heart — and no one there to save me, with sex or conversation.

This pain of separateness could teach me something. Like a pain in the body, I can acknowledge it or deny it, deal with the symptom or the cause. Doctors give us antibiotics and our bodies lose the strength to fight infection on their own. So have I relied on women: not to do my laundry or cook for me, but to protect me from the thoughts and feelings that hurt the most; to cushion the heart from grief — for a dead son or a dead father — and from the daily, unremembered disappointments; to save me from my own judgments, the iron opinions, the certainties forever changing.

This is bitter medicine. My ego doesn't want to swallow it. It would rather go on lying to itself until one day I wake up with cancer. Does that sound melodramatic? I think every psychological ailment has its physical counterpart; the distinction between the two exists only in our fragmented mind, and may not show up for a while. But we're far more unified than medical science imagines. Our bodies are capable of healing themselves, if only we trust their deep wisdom. What are we, anyway, but the signature of spirit in flesh? Why would spirit forge its name? Why should we be incomplete, needing knives to cut us, pills to cure us, someone always to hold our hand?

DROPPING OUT

I SAW A MOVIE RECENTLY about a young couple who decide to quit their jobs and spend the rest of their lives roaming around the country. They encounter one mishap after another, losing almost all their money as well as their illusions. Their odyssey is short-lived; eventually, they go back to their old jobs. Escape just isn't possible, the movie is saying. Dropping out is as ludicrous a dream as the lives we want to drop out from.

For Hollywood, such cynicism isn't surprising; still, the movie troubled me, reminding me of my own life, my longing to be free. Years ago, I decided to escape, too, from a whole way of life, its worries and its comforts, its cruel mortgaging of the present to the future. I wanted to create something different for myself, paying as I went, writing no checks my heart couldn't cover, giving up a good living for a good life.

We'd been planning the getaway for more than a year, reading travel books, studying maps, going to the bank every Friday with our two paychecks (my wife was a teacher, I was a newspaper reporter) to deposit one in our checking account and the other in savings. Judy and I knew something was missing from our lives, though we had no idea what it might be. We were both good at what we did; we had master's degrees from prestigious universities and the kind of savvy that makes getting ahead less a challenge than a social obligation — the shelf of your life cleared for the trophies the future will surely bestow.

I'd already won some awards, and displayed them proudly in the hallway next to my degrees — the same hallway I'd pace at night after getting home from work, not knowing what to do with myself, feeling hemmed in by our small apartment, and hemmed in too by the world's most exciting city, having had enough remarkable meals in enough intimate restaurants, and hemmed in most of all by my own restlessness, which I couldn't even name, like some hauntingly familiar melody that had become the soundtrack of my days.

I wanted a change. I wanted to take a giant leap away from everything familiar: my job, the city, the weekly visits to my parents' house to argue with my father, the friends whose lives were turning into success stories whose endings I could guess. I needed to say goodbye to all that.

In 1969 we sailed for Europe. It took five days, but that was the idea: I wanted the sense of making a great passage, of crossing an ocean, of journeying not just through time but through space. How often we measure distances, even the greatest distances, in hours. Instead, I wanted wave upon endless wave, the luminescent greens and blues, the darkest of darks lapping against the giant hull, as the ship carried us forward into the night and the next day and the next night, making time itself unreal. I wanted a passage through the mind, a beginning, a birth — but of what, I couldn't say. Standing by the rail, looking across the watery nothingness, I was staring as well into my own life. We had sold the car and the furniture, quit our jobs, put all the money in traveler's checks. To leave behind nearly everything that made up our life was exhilarating and terrifying. I wondered how a blind man might feel being helped across the street by a total stranger. What trust I had placed in a part of me I knew nothing about! More than once, I asked myself if it wasn't too late to turn back.

We docked in Southampton, England, and rented a car for the drive to London. "It keeps stalling," I told the man at the counter. He walked outside and stood beside the car while I tried again. I turned the key, shifted clumsily, gave it some gas, and again it stalled. "The brake," he said. I stared at him, confused. "The brake," he repeated politely. "You need to take off the brake." Accustomed to cars with automatic transmissions, I hadn't even looked at the brake. I smiled sheepishly, thanked him, coaxed the gearshift into first, and pulled directly into a lane of oncoming traffic — forgetting, in my embarrassment, to keep to the left. I swerved, eased the car into second, but when I tried to shift to third, the gearshift wouldn't budge. As we coasted along at twenty-five miles an hour, everyone passed us but no one blew his horn. How extravagantly courteous! How disconcerting! How I yearned for the rudeness of a New York cabbie.

Don't we often ache for what's familiar, even when it's painful? I've read that battered children sometimes reach out to their parents as they're being carried to safety. How I longed for the home I'd been counting the days to leave. I felt uncommonly estranged here, and my mood of displacement only deepened as our travels continued. I realized, after a few months, that it had less to do with the eerie beauty and dinginess of the cities, the nuances of custom, the attitudes that changed like the landscape, or the languages that rose and fell across the centuries of shared history, than with a different migration altogether, the journey I had begun within myself, which was moving me beyond my borders.

I was becoming less sure of who I was. How could I convincingly call myself a journalist, since I wasn't writing, or a New Yorker, since I had no address, or even a resentful son, since I was no longer losing ridiculous arguments? The backstage door was swinging open, and the troupe of selves I called me was breaking up, leaving like actors at the end of the show. The old lines weren't working anymore.

There were, of course, other, more obvious changes: my hair started curling down past my neck, and soon reached my shoulders; instead of dressing each day in a suit and tie, I wore jeans and a leather vest; I carried a shoulder bag rather than an attache case, and though I kept a pipe inside, just like in the old days, it wasn't for tobacco. Some of these changes were purely symbolic: I'd never cared for long hair on men, but it wasn't just hair; it was a flag, a sign of my independence. Some of the changes were for convenience: since we were living in a van and camping out, dressing casually made sense. Yet other changes spoke of deeper stirrings: using drugs helped me clear the rubble around my heart, even if the flowers that grew in the cracks were short-lived.

My besieged ego latched on to these changes. Here, at least, was the outline of an identity. Being a hippie had never been my ambition, but it was better than nothing; to my ego, anything was better than nothing. For without the armor of an identity, I was defenseless against myself — which is to say, my own pain and confusion. Always, I had read the newspapers carefully; could I bear to read between the lines of my own life with such scrutiny? Where inside myself was the peace I wanted to see on earth? Could I forgive my father for bullying me? Could I forgive myself for bullying my wife? Could I even think about these things for more than a few seconds without reaching for the door? When your face in the mirror becomes a headline your heart can't bear, when you see how much of your life is a monument to fear, and there's no one left to blame, no parent or teacher or boss, indeed not even yourself, then the desire to escape becomes overwhelming. There are many exits, plainly marked; pretending you know who you are is one of them.

We stayed in Europe for two years, then headed back to America in search of the ideal commune. By this time, we'd become acquainted with Eastern religion, which my ego had turned into another prize. Now, I was someone spiritual. Now, I was on the path. Now that I knew we were all one, I could use that knowledge, too, to set myself apart.

This is a country with a tradition of rebellion; ever since the Boston Tea Party, every generation has staked its claim to something a little nobler or fairer or sweeter than what came before. Had I come of age in the thirties, I probably would have become a Marxist; in the forties, a hipster; in the fifties, a beatnik. No doubt, I would have been tempted to define myself narrowly then, too. What is more seductive, after all, than the mind's whisper that it's the form that counts: what you do, where you live, how you look. But there's no form, in the system or out of it, that guarantees happiness or justice or salvation. Look at organized religion. Look at the rebel leaders after they win power. Look behind the curtains of every life that proclaims an easy path to glory, freedom without a price.

Look at my life now: independent, uncompromised, a living example of the best of the ideals I struggled all those years to attain. But don't miss the small print, the warning that living all your ideals may be dangerous to your health. My friends joke about how early I get up, how hard I work. I make a joke of it myself, because I'd rather hear their laughter than their admonitions, their reminders of what I know yet every day forget: that if I get too caught up in getting things done, I end up sabotaging what I cherish the most. How easy to create suffering while trying to save the world. How tempting to tyrannize myself, to dictate goals, instead of risking real democracy, true self-government. The runner gets out for half an hour a day, but the poet has been under house arrest since last August and the contemplative who originally lobbied for getting up early, so there would be time to meditate before going to work, is hooted down now, denounced as a malingerer. Why sit for twenty minutes doing nothing, the boss wants to know.

If my life looks the same as that of any overwrought executive; if the most serious writing I get to most mornings is my list of things to do; if I swill coffee; if I go away to the beach for the weekend, taking with me two boxes of unread magazines (telling my wife, with a straight face, this would be a good chance for me to catch up); if I continue to pretend I'm ever going to catch up by working a little harder; if I think of vacations as needing to be earned; if I again and again confuse fulfillment with the form of things, rather than remembering it's my own awareness that gives meaning to the form — then what am I to do? Sell the car and the furniture and set off on another journey in search of myself? Drop out again? Can you drop out of dropping out?

When I was in Europe, I heard of an American who would live in a country until he started to understand the language, then move to another country until he learned the language there. Each time he moved, it was said, he realized people were talking the same bullshit as everywhere else.

Where is there to go when you're always bringing yourself along? What novelty doesn't wear off? To drop out of society — that's the easy part, like stepping off a cliff. To land on your feet, to keep the ground of your humanness under you — that's the work of a lifetime, not a lifestyle, and it's the work I find hardest of all.

GENERATIONS

I'M BEING AS QUIET AS I CAN. The children are asleep in the next room and I don't want to wake them. I thought of going to the office for a while, getting back before they wake up, but even when they're asleep I want to be near them. The time together is so brief: one week each month. I keep thinking this will get easier. It does, in a way. We get used to everything.

I listen to their breathing, study their small bodies curved with sleep's signature — Mara with one arm over her head, extravagantly trusting; Sara curled up like a flower that closes at night. Already, Sara doesn't remember her dreams, or chooses not to tell them. I cover them with the sheet, smooth their hair, moving over them like a dream.

It's been six years since their mother and I split up. Missing them is as familiar to me as they are; I can't imagine life without them, or without the pain of being without them. It's as unarguable as breathing in and out. Yet sometimes I want to hold my breath, breathe in the smell of them, never let go.

All parents know the feeling: their child's first day at school, their first night sleeping at a friend's house, their first date. A goodbye is a goodbye. It's just that I say so damned many of them. The phrase "broken family" isn't heard these days. Joint custody, shared parenting — these are the euphemisms. But the human heart hasn't changed. You can break a glass once. You can break a leg several times. But the heart breaks and breaks and breaks. A broken family *is* a broken heart.

I wonder if even in the best of circumstances — a happy marriage, every kind of security — there's anything harder than being a parent. To be a friend, a lover, a husband or a wife, these raise us high and bring us low, unfurl the heart like a banner and snap it in the wind. But to be a parent — well, as our parents told us, you need to be one to know. Nothing calls to us so unmistakably by our true name, like a bell ringing in the mind, awakening us from our dream of self, forcing us out of ourselves, to give and give again — usually without thanks, but that doesn't matter when the giving is real.

Is there anything that comes close for grief and joy? Only one thing: being a child. That's the knot no one unties. No matter how old we are, we're always someone's child. If you want to know who you really are, just weigh what's important: put race, religion, economics, I.Q. on one side of the scale, your parents on the other. There's no question which way it will tip.

This night, standing over my sleeping children, I'm standing, for a moment, between generations. My mother is coming, for her first visit in more than two years. I'm wondering if this will be the same visit the two of us have had again and again. After Mara and Sara's prodigious accomplishment in growing a few more inches has been duly marveled at and praised; after the gifts have been opened; after the reminiscences, the stories, the gossip, the jokes; after the round of silly hometown boosterism (she, with her New York accent, telling me how great it is in California, where she now lives; I, with my New York accent, insisting it's just as swell here in North Carolina); after all this, the table cleared, the novelty of being together wearing off, I wonder: will we face each other as strangers again? Will we argue, as we've always argued, about why we don't love each other more? Will we eye each other with blame? And, because we never get anywhere, will we then ignore what was and wasn't said, talk some more about the children, tell the favorite stories again, until it's time, in another day or two, to drive her to the airport, time for another goodbye?

It doesn't start well. My sister and her husband are supposed to drive my mother here from Virginia, where she's been visiting them. When she comes East, she always visits my sister first, and stays with her longer. Do I resent this? It's like resenting a mountain. From the very beginning they were closer. It was part of the unquestioned landscape of my childhood.

How much else I took for granted. I had two sets of parents — my parents and my father's parents — which didn't seem strange to me. The rivalries were ferocious, recriminations darkening the air. My grandmother ruled, even from her invalid's bed. Proud, domineering, she was an Old World matriarch; one moment she'd praise you, the next moment she'd bully and blame. Long ago, she'd convinced my father he was responsible for her suffering; I was taught the same. With her raging diabetes and arthritic knees, she was dependent on my mother's care. She resented her, belittled her. My mother had nowhere to turn. She felt duty-bound, trapped, a victim. Even the small joys of motherhood were denied her: she'd fill the bath and my grandmother would bathe me; she'd prepare the food and my grandmother would feed me. My mother says I was taken from her. Taken or given — for me, the hurt was the same.

When my sister was born, my mother decided it wouldn't happen again.

So where are they? I thought they'd be here early. Isn't that what my sister said on the phone? We eat without them. We let the children stay up late. Finally, a call. They just got into town. Do we want to meet them for dinner?

Apparently, we misunderstood each other. I try to keep the disappointment and irritation out of my voice, but I'm not completely successful. My mother is hurt that I'm hurt. I tell her to forget it, it's not important.

We end up meeting later on, at her motel. Mara and Sara are obviously excited; I'm struck by their open-hearted acceptance of her. Perhaps I should emulate my children. But it's not that easy. Our parents are not just other people. We share with them a deep, intimate, and often painful history. Their confusions, all the sorry deals they made, become our inheritance. As a parent, I know this;

it's humbling. I try to be a better parent. But whatever is still dark and unexplored in me casts its shadow over my children. It's hard to face such a harsh fact. My mother can't. To her, acknowledging this legacy, passed from generation to generation, is too painful. She feels blamed.

I understand this, too. (It's amazing how understanding I can be when I'm writing.) It's hard not to succumb to guilt when faced with our own frailties. Being a parent, regularly failing, shows us over and over how human we are. It takes a big heart to love ourselves in spite of this.

My mother gives the girls their gifts: dolls, pocketbooks, stationery, socks. Lots of socks, thirty or forty pairs. (She's in the business.) Her pleasure in giving them things is genuine. But after the gifts are opened, the excitement ends, and she doesn't quite know what to do. They're her grandchildren while they're opening gifts. They're strangers, really, when they're not playing that role.

We spend the next day at the motel pool, Mara and Sara in the water, my mother and I talking. Years ago, it was my habit to bring up the past. I was trying to unravel who I was. I imagined that confronting her with my hurt and anger would be healing, perhaps for both of us. I was wrong. Reconciling myself with the past doesn't mean she and I have to agree on what happened.

But now she wants to talk about it. For several years, she's had cancer. Chemotherapy has kept it under control and there's been little pain, but emotionally it's been a struggle. She's about to begin taking drugs again, and she's afraid.

She asks me to tell her that I love her, to show her that I do, so that I won't feel guilty for missing the chance while she was still alive. I don't know what to say. The poignant scene she's asking for isn't in me. We never were very affectionate. She rarely kissed or hugged me when I was a child. When I asked her about this a few years ago, she explained, "I'm not a physically affectionate person." I want to leap over my hesitation, reach out to her reassuringly and tell her she's loved. But I'm walking on broken glass. I've swept and swept, and still there's more.

"Why do you still blame me?" she asks. I tell her it's not easy to separate who she is now from who she was then. "That's OK," she says. "I can take it. It doesn't matter anyway." It's obvious it does matter. I try to get her to admit that, but she won't. A moment later, though, she's in tears. "Why won't you love me?" It's heart-wrenching. I know what she's asking for, and I can't give it. I feel my guilt rising. This is my *mother*! How can I be so cruel? Then I remind myself I'm not being cruel. I didn't create this emptiness in her and I can't fill it. To try isn't love, it's madness.

Of course, I tell myself later, I could have tried harder. Surely, amidst all the emotional lies and half-truths of my childhood, there were moments of genuine love. Why can't I forgive her for the rest? Why can't I hug her and say, with conviction, "It's all right. You did your best. I know how hard it was. I understand." Because I do understand: about her mother, who worked all day and didn't have time for the children at night; her father with the wild temper who "prayed like a crazy person"; the poverty; the fear of men; the marriage that allowed her to escape only to another prison; the pregnancy; the twelve-hour labor; the little boy in her arms crying, needing, needing what she couldn't give.

I understand and still there's this wound. The salves I apply — sex, words, spiritual accomplishment — don't heal it. Yet if I blame her, I need to blame her parents, too. And their parents. And theirs. We're all lost in our separateness. It's the darkest, deepest well. The cup is passed from one generation to the next.

When I was seven or eight, she was in her mid-thirties, just a few years younger than I am now. I remember seeing a photograph of her, a new one. I was stunned — the glow of her cheeks, her kind eyes, the flower in her hair. I'd never seen her with a flower in her hair. I thought she was the most beautiful woman in the world.

It's one of many images of her I carry within me. Some are beautiful, and some aren't. It's ironic: the less I deny the painful memories, the more real she becomes for me, not just as an imperfect mother but as a woman rich in contradictions, exquisitely complex. This is what she wants, isn't it? But I can't give it to her yet. Whenever I take a detour around grief, I end up lost. Whenever I scold myself for not being more loving, I end up incapable of love. Forgiveness is important, but it's not some accomplishment, some lofty goal. It's what's waiting for me after I'm done with the blame. It waits like a mother with her arms outstretched. Only I can't run to her. I must keep walking, step by step.

ADDING ON

I'M STANDING on a makeshift scaffold, about ten feet in the air. Not very high, really, looked at from below. Up here, though, perched on these rickety boards, I feel like I'm standing in a canoe. George says it's perfectly safe, with the infuriating casualness of someone who thinks everything is. But I'm worried that a board will break, followed by a leg or a neck. Or, since the boards aren't nailed to anything, that I'll step too close to the edge and, like some cartoon character, seesaw into space — too short a journey for my life to pass before me in satisfying detail.

Yet I need to go higher to wedge this heavy crowbar under the wooden siding I'm ripping off the house. I climb on the sawhorse we've dragged up here for that purpose. Despite my wife's steadying hand, it's rickety, too.

I pry out some nails, yank another board loose. The sound of wood and nail being separated is like some deep groaning in the chest of the house — a mournful sound, but music to me: one less board to tear off.

My wife isn't happy up here either; she's always been afraid of heights. So, of course, we joke — about this ludicrous perch, about falling, about the work we've taken on, its pleasures and risks. I have a band-aid on my finger, another on my toe. There are cuts on my face and legs and several black-and-blue marks of mysterious origin. Norma is bruised, too. But our worst welts have been raised with words. Oh, the arguing. About nothing, everything. I'm told it's in the nature of this work, this building of a home. But there are no lovers' spats on scaffolds. Up in the air, we're friends again.

We started only recently on the addition, which nearly doubles the size of our small house. Notwithstanding our inexperience, we've made remarkable progress, struggling with each other and with these heavy two-by-tens that must be coaxed inch by inch into place. All the metaphors of heart and home join as neatly as boards cut to fit, joining us in frustration and pride and the sweat of our brow — no small thing, either, on these near-100 degree days.

Supposedly, we're doing the work ourselves to save money, but I think the real reason is to save something of ourselves, something to draw on when times get rough, a recollection of effort that paid off, of something built true, of cuts that healed.

Getting things done, physically, gives me more satisfaction than I would have imagined. There's no mental substitute — no matter how rich the mix of ideas. It doesn't matter how simple the accomplishment: sawing something down the middle, or joining two boards with a nail and making what was separate one. As I become more skilled, I become more daring. I imagine I can learn to do anything, to trust tools and to trust my steady hands, to design my wild dreams and build them, to climb high, higher.

George comes out nearly every day. A friend of a friend, he's a builder of more than thirty years' experience, a generous man who is helping us as a favor.

We're an odd match. Imagine Ronald Reagan and Jesse Jackson; imagine night and day. George has built nuclear reactors and believes in them fiercely. We stay away from this and other subjects the way I'd stay away from Three Mile Island. After all, I have plenty of friends who share my most impassioned opinions; we can have an orgy of agreement any day at the natural foods restaurant, over a sprout sandwich. But he's the one out here helping.

George believes in helping people help themselves, even Yankees like me. (I've lived in the South many years, but that doesn't matter; the highest compliment George has paid me is, "For a guy from Brooklyn, there may be hope for you yet.") On the way to a nearby sawmill, he holds forth on a favorite topic: the greed of the lumber companies. For example, a so-called two-by-ten, he explains (as he has explained several times before, but he is passionate about the subject) really measures about one-and-three-quarters by nine-and-a-half, after the rough-sawn wood has been smoothed. "You're paying for the sawdust," he says. By going directly to a sawmill, we're saving money and "getting what we pay for."

At the mill, after we've loaded up, the owner walks over to say hello. Pointing to the lumber in the truck, he asks, "You know how wide those are?" The question is rhetorical, unembarrassed boasting. "Get your tape and measure it," he says. George obliges. "Ten inches exact," George says, and the owner beams.

"I told you," George tells me on the way back.

It's hot, very hot. At night, the heat is a blanket you can't throw off. At noon, it's the whip on the slave's back. Can you imagine, I ask Norma — the sweat pouring off me, running down my arm, down the hammer, falling like tears — being in the fields in this heat ten, twelve hours a day, unable to take a break when you want, go inside for a cold drink? Of course, we can't imagine. We are always mistaking the suffering of others; it's either much worse than we think or not nearly so bad. Such a deep pocket, human nature. You put your hand in and there's no telling what you'll find.

Down the road from us live a half-dozen black families, and one white man, described to us as a redneck, but I decide to wait and see. One morning, we stop the car, get out and introduce ourselves. I joke, ingratiatingly, about being the new hippies, and he laughs. Yet, within minutes, he's complaining about "the nigger" who didn't show up to do some work for him, how "lazy" he is. The comment is abrupt, uncalled for, yet clearly important for him to get across, a way of naming himself, turning out his pockets, the way others let on in a hurry they know Christ, or where to get cocaine. We listen, not saying much; the talk turns to crops, to the heat.

Our road is easy to find but our house, a twisting half-mile down the road, is not. Have faith, I tell friends when I give them directions, yet nearly all who come out imagine they've gotten lost, just before finding us.

Once they've gotten here, there's no question it's the right place — the construction materials lined up perfectly, every board stacked neatly, little piles of scrap wood set apart from other little piles, laughably orderly, like my desk, my closets, the refrigerator shelves. Some people, when they feel insecure, go out and spend money, or have a drink, or call a friend. I tidy up. Norma is usually good-natured about it, but I know I'm hard to live with. I'm as extreme as some unregenerate slob.

Naturally I'm dismayed when the carpenters show up to help with the framing. I can tell from the start these guys don't arrange their home libraries in alphabetical order. As unobtrusively as possible, I pick up after them: saws, cigarette butts, soda cans. "Nice place you got here," one of them says, flinging a two-by-four into the strawberry patch.

The next day, the carpenters don't show up at all. George, who had arranged for them to work this weekend, apologizes. "Carpenters are never dependable," he says. Besides, one of them has "a domineering wife, who probably decided for the both of them to take a trip." I wonder whether this woman is domineering or simply speaks her mind, and whether to George, that's the same.

And what about me? I keep encouraging Norma to express her feelings boldly and without compromise, which is difficult for her, she says. My advice sounds sincere, even to me — yet why have I always married shy women, whom I then implore to be less shy?

Once again, the carpenters don't show. What was supposed to be easy — paying someone to do the framing and roofing — turns out to be hard. We're no good at waiting. I'm disappointed but don't acknowledge it; I don't want George to think I'm unappreciative. Norma is openly impatient and I become impatient with her impatience, giving her a little lecture on nonattachment.

To save money, we shop for used doors and windows. We find five windows for only five dollars each, which we buy from a doctor's wife who has just remodeled, bargaining with her as we stand in the rain. But we can't find the right door. We discover one we like at an antique store — solid oak, with stained glass, exquisitely crafted — but, at twelve hundred dollars, it's a little out of our range.

So was our house, but friends loaned us the money for the down payment and the addition, and the owner, also a friend, agreed to finance the purchase herself. Our monthly payments for the house and seven acres are less than most people pay for a two-bedroom apartment in town. Still, we both feel some embarrassment at owning land, as if it makes us seem more prosperous than we actually are, or more bourgeois, or more "adult" — though, at thirty-nine, I don't know what I'm waiting for.

ASHES TO ASHES

I F I STILL HAD THEM, they'd be yellowing by now, like leaves, turning dry and curling at the edge: the letters; the photographs; the yearbooks; the oversized, preposterously formal "lawyer's diary" my father proudly handed me on my eighth birthday, whose high, important pages indifferently bore my little entries, crowded together at the top; the heavenly face of Barbara Katz, the first girl I truly loved (and thus passionately and loudly insisted I hated), there, in the third row, over on the left, of my sixth-grade class picture; the high-school newspaper that carried my first byline, raised like a flag on a new land.

If I still had them, how often would I look at them? Not very often, I think. Probably, they'd sit untouched, in a box, in a closet, yet there might be satisfaction in that. How like leaves our memories are, strewn across the past, so easily scattered — and thus we rake them, into albums, scrapbooks, letters saved.

Time carries away so much; we've lost so much: it's natural to want to preserve the past. Yet how sentimental these thoughts would have seemed to me that night, thirteen years ago, when I tried to erase the past. Such a strange night, spent huddled around the fireplace with two friends in that crumbling mansion we shared. Such a cold night, in that old barn of a house, ghostly with its own histories, its elegant bygone days, its slave shacks out back. Such a long night, as the wind rattled the windows, and the flames leapt higher each time one of us threw something in: Cindy's journals; hundreds of photographs Ken had taken; the short stories I'd written the year before. The albums, the scrapbooks, the letters — one by one, I burned them all. Almost in a kind of spell, under the sway of a man I'd never met, challenged and perplexed by his odd ideas, I thought I was erasing my personal history, setting myself free.

Thirteen years later, as I mourn the loss of the things I burned, and realize with hindsight that don Juan, the great Yaqui Indian teacher I was trying to emulate, would only have scoffed at me, it's tempting for me to scoff, too. At my naiveté. My spiritual pride. My faith in ideas I read about in books. But for all my regrets, I'm still moved by the memory of that night, and its enduring lessons for me.

Of the many ideas I'd encountered in Carlos Castaneda's books about don Juan — who initiated Castaneda into a new way of seeing as a "man of knowledge" — the concept of erasing personal history touched me, that dreary winter, the most deeply.

Like Castaneda, I had a strong attachment to my past. I could keenly imagine his discomfort when don Juan chided him for believing that, without a sense of continuity, life had no purpose, and for telling his friends and family everything he did.

"Your trouble," don Juan scolded, "is that you have to explain everything to everybody, compulsively, and at the same time you want to keep the freshness, the newness of what you do."

A true spiritual warrior needs to be transparent to himself and to others, don Juan maintained, so no one can pin him down with their thoughts.

"What's wrong is that once they know you," he continued, "you are an affair taken for granted and from that moment on you won't be able to break the tie of their thoughts. I personally like the ultimate freedom of being unknown. No one knows me with steadfast certainty, the way people know you. . . .

"You see," he went on, "we have only two alternatives: we either take everything for sure and real, or we don't. If we follow the first, we end up bored to death with ourselves and with the world. If we follow the second and erase personal history, we create a fog around us, a very exciting and mysterious state in which nobody knows exactly where the rabbit will pop out, not even ourselves."

Erasing personal history was, just then, appealing. Within the past year, New Eden, the rural commune my first wife and I had moved to North Carolina to join, had failed and was abandoned; our son, born prematurely, had lived only three days; then our marriage had died. Having left a promising career in journalism for the uncertain rewards of going back to the land, I was now without a farm or a family or a future. Trying to explain what had happened — not just to friends and family but, in an unceasing inner monologue, to myself — only added to my sorrow. It was easy to see that I was recreating my painful history every time I talked about it.

I knew that burning old albums and scrapbooks and letters wouldn't in itself erase the memories. Nor would I miraculously stop thinking or talking about myself. The fire was, instead, a symbolic act. I yearned to be a spiritual warrior: free of the past, free of pride and guilt, free of routines; unpredictable, triumphant over my fears. I knew it wouldn't be easy, which was all the more reason to make a dramatic gesture — if not, like Castaneda, on some high, rugged mountain swept by raging winds, then in my own way, in the way of my fathers, with a sacrifice and a prayer.

Like me, my housemates were eager seekers after truth. I'd only recently met them and they'd offered me a room in their house, where we were sitting that evening, talking about what it meant to erase the past. Someone was telling a story and, in the middle of it, threw something, a letter or a photograph, into the flames. It burned furiously for a moment and then, like the past, was gone. In silence, we stared at the fire for a while, then looked at each other conspiratorially, our imaginations kindled by the act.

All night, the flames continued to dance, our faces animated by the fire's glow and by our own changing expressions, as we unburdened ourselves of our things and the stories they held. Was there an emotion not felt that night as we relived and tried to release the past? Anger, sadness, joy, longing — they rose like mingled breath, they curled like smoke. We let them drift away from us, these stories, these souvenirs, hoping that a future awaited us which was more stupendous and unfathomable than our scrapbooks could possibly suggest.

How many trips we made the next day, hauling out the ashes. How many times I've sifted through those ashes in my mind, trying to understand what was lost that night and what, if anything, was gained.

It wasn't the first and it wouldn't be the last time I'd fervently imagine that a single act would redeem me. Many times I've wanted to believe that my life was nothing but a prelude to one fateful moment: the lightning insight, the trumpet, the guru's touch. I've believed that my life needed to be redeemed, forgiven, made whole.

I still do. But I no longer insist it occur in a blinding flash. There are moments of illumination, during which I'm reminded of what real clarity and compassion are: they come in dreams, or sometimes with drugs, or perhaps most profoundly, when I'm in the deepest despair. I've cried out, and my cry has been answered — but life, with all its contradictions and ambiguities, hasn't ended there. The thirsty man drinks and gets thirsty again. Richard Bach, in *Illusions*, asks how you're able to figure out when your work on earth is ended. "If you're alive," he answers, "it isn't."

If our work here is to understand who we really are — to uncover, painstakingly, like archaeologists sifting through dust, what is buried and hidden in each of us — then what's gained by denying anything that's a part of me? Isn't that a way of clinging to it all the more? The letters and photographs and albums are ashes now, even the ashes are gone, but are the memories? Where could they possibly go? Where does the present moment go? And when it returns as a memory, whispering tenderly, or pounding with its terrible fist, is it still the past? When personal history repeats itself — when I realize I've made the same mistake I've made countless times before — am I diminished by it? When I glimpse, in my daughter's face, the shadow of my own, or hear her ask the same question I asked my father, and also never got a good answer for, does this bind me to something dead and best forgotten? I think not; I think instead it creates some humility in me, and perhaps, as a result, a different future for her.

It's not the past I want to drop now, but my habit of diminishing the fullness of what I've experienced. For what are most of our stories but cartoon versions of the past? Our personal history is the well-worn version of ourselves we've settled for, in which we come across as pitiful stick figures, "bored to death with ourselves and with the world," as don Juan said.

In retrospect, burning all my things seems less like an act of liberation than of oppression — like the Nazis burning books in a tortured attempt to redeem a culture by destroying its inner life, its history of ideas, its rich and varied past.

I received a letter recently from a friend who no longer reads my writing because, she says, it's too negative. She scolds me for dwelling on the past, "the ancestors, the relatives, the critical and condemning friends, the little boy who cries in the dark. Give him a quarter and tell him to go to the movies."

She reminds me I'm free to create my own reality if I throw away my garments of mourning and live in the present. "Please wrap your heart in ribbons," she says, "and let the wind blow through your hair. . . ."

Her advice seems facile and a little unkind, but is it any different from what I once asked of myself? I know how tempting it is to want to be done with the past, to vanquish what I haven't been able to accept. I can feel her frustration at my not having forgiven myself my too-human failings; she says she forgave me long ago.

Shall I tell her that of course I want to live in the present — but if I don't truly accept the past (and sometimes that means talking to myself or others about it, recreating it so I might better understand it, and even mourning it), then the present becomes a race in which I'm always trying to keep one step ahead of my partialness and my pain?

Shall I tell her I wrote this because I've never forgiven myself the mistake I made so many years ago? Letting myself mourn what was lost then, in my vain attempt to be free of myself, has helped me to accept that night.

PORNOGRAPHY'S CHILD

I DISCOVERED SEX IN 1955, in a hatbox, in my father's closet.

What a cache he kept there, beneath the gabardine business suits and woolen overcoats and wide flowering ties, draped like jungle foliage over a metal rack; the closet smelling vaguely of him, his cigars, his aftershave, and my mother's mothballs, although the books crammed into that hatbox had a different smell entirely: funky, spicy, foreign (written in English, they were published in France). For years, I imagined sex would smell that way, too.

They were odd little books, crudely printed, as if on a press that hadn't been cleaned in years, the letters fat and smudged, the photographs grainy. And the prices! I don't know which astounded me more: what was in them, or the fact that they cost at least ten dollars each. I'd been amassing an enviable science fiction collection for fifty cents a book. It was inconceivable to me that anyone would charge, or my father would pay, that much money for something like this.

But there was nothing like this, was there? These stories and pictures puzzled and enchanted me. I studied the photographs the way a botanist might look at a plant he had no idea existed. I mean, it didn't seem quite real, though the evidence was compelling: all the naked bodies, joined hip to hip, or mouth to crotch, in threesomes and foursomes, in beds, leaning over chairs — apparently enjoying themselves, though that was suggested more by the text than the often bored and distracted faces. All this hothouse groping and moaning, long-voweled ahhs and ohhs: unbelievable, but here it was. People actually did this; at least, they did it for the camera.

I was ten years old, just starting the sixth grade, and had never been told a thing about sex. This was an era, remember, when *sex* and *education* did not roll off the tongue as if they were one word, but seemed to be at opposite ends of the universe, separated by worlds of ignorance and embarrassment and denial. Like the lens

of a telescope, these books let me see (and in such detail!) un-
dreamt planets — though I was still unsure it wasn't just more
science fiction. It took my classmate Eddie to ignite the real rocket
of my curiosity with the casual disclosure, on the P.S. 244
schoolyard, that "fucking makes babies."

Oh the lightning leap my mind took, synapses quivering and
bucking, revelation rolling in like a thunderclap: people really *did*
do this; it wasn't just something they conjured up in France for my
father's amusement.

I soon discovered that the pleasures the books so abundantly
described were, after a fashion, available to me, too — if not at the
crossroads of male and female (which would have required a bit of
social engineering beyond my capacity), then at the juncture, surely
no less steamy, of my hand and my imagination.

For the first time since I was three, I started taking afternoon
naps — in my parents' bedroom. It was, I explained, quieter up
there. Of course, I hardly slept at all. I read and re-read; in a lifetime of reading have I ever come across anything so crude and so
compelling? There was no pretense here of literature, of feathery
description, of artful erotica. The only artistry was that of my own
touch: the book propped up on the bed so both hands could be
free, my fingers making a music all their own. Never mind the
hack lyrics: between my legs, the symphony swelled and moaned,
lifting me high and higher; teasing with a soft note; bringing me
down with a groan.

Amazingly, I was never discovered. Or maybe it's not so amazing, as we always learn what we must to survive. In that household,
stealth was as necessary as it would be to a hunter crouching in the
woods — or, more to the point, to his prey. When it came to sex,
none of us got downwind of each other. But that was true of most
things. For all the arguing, the unrelieved histrionics, there was
little real feeling expressed in my family. There were words, and
more words, in two languages yet (my father's parents, who spoke

Yiddish, lived with us), but the language of pure emotion, the only language the heart understands, wasn't spoken. Instead of hurt honestly stated, there was anger; instead of anger, there was envy; instead of doubt, there was debate. And instead of sex, there was secrecy and silence. So I covered my tracks — indeed, I did a better job than my father had — put back the books, wiped off the stains.

Thirty years later, I'm still covering my tracks, but from whom? In a sexually enlightened age, why the secrecy about my longings, as if sex and pornography were the same, and my dirty thoughts best kept in a closet? Why, after all the marriages and affairs, after all the sex — dry humps and sloppy wet reunions, puppy dog sex and shark sex, pinball sex, saintly sex, psychedelic melt-your-heart sex — why, after all this sex, am I still ashamed about sex? Why, when I look at a woman, does the guilt follow so quickly upon the desire that the two have become indistinguishable? Indeed, after all the women I've seen, in the flesh and in my own imagination, why am I looking at all?

In the current debate over pornography, I would be an ideal witness for either side.

The civil libertarians could put me on the stand to wave the flag of freedom — and a patriot I am, ready to die for those jewels in the American crown, our First Amendment rights. The book-burners, on the other hand, could simply take judge and jury on a tour of my ruins, letting the facts speak for themselves, letting my false hungers and false gods betray me. Step closer, your honor. Oh sisters of mercy, gather round. Justice, raise your blindfold, and look, if you can, at this sorry desolation: the mind turned into a Hollywood set, its windows taped over with stills. Women in every possible pose, in every shade of desire, wanting him, or coyly pretending not to, showing him what he wants to see, or shimmering for a moment in the distance, always out of reach, a mirage. But isn't it all illusion?

Look at him — once a boy who stared in wonder at the stars, who knew before any of his friends the names of all the planets — look at him, now trembling with anticipation over the darkened line where panties meet thigh. What does he see there with his tortured eyes? The violence, your honor! Not just to women — oh no — but to this young boy's soul, his innocence drawn from him as surely as he dreams of his seed being drawn out by one of those fancy French tongues. And now he's lived his dreams. He's fully a man. And what licks at him, my judge — my dark judge, my stern judge — is fire. Isn't he a victim, too?

Victim, oppressor. It's a razor line between. A friend tells me he buys men's magazines so he can masturbate while looking at the pictures, but he feels guilty for supporting an industry that exploits women. I tell him that once in a while I buy those magazines, too — sneakily, with an alibi prepared should someone I know see me in the store. We laugh, and I wonder if this is how prisoners laugh, fingering the bars. But aren't we the tower guards, too, peering down at the women in the yard? It's a substitute for intimacy, he says. A sorry substitute, I reply. At least it's safe, he says. Safe, I agree, but less interesting than the real thing. Even when there's a woman in his life, he says, he buys the magazines. Well, I say, I can understand that. I'm happily married, and sometimes I masturbate, too, but never happily. If I'm not, in my fantasy, exploiting a *Penthouse* model, or a movie star, or a friend, I'm surely exploiting myself, turning sex once again into porn.

Ah, the guilt. It's even more relentless than the horniness. Like an eager lover, it prods all night at the heart. And what, exactly, am I so guilty about? Is it my desire, or is it my denial of my desire, or both? One moment, I'll berate myself for my insatiable sexual appetite. The next, I'll malign myself for my mousy heart, for laundering my dirty thoughts with spirituality or fidelity ("sex is wrong except with *her*") instead of telling the world what I really worship and what I'm really married to: the pursuit of my own pleasure. But then I feel guilty for describing myself so crudely, and thus distorting my deeper longings, which sex only masks. Isn't that pornographic, too, to titillate myself with a version of myself barren of soul, as if *I* were the centerfold — a staple through the navel, the pages of my days sticky with passion's passionate lies?

Perhaps I'm being too hard on myself. We all make a pornographic movie of the world, objectifying ourselves, emphasizing fear instead of love, jerking off into images of comfort or fame or money — or sex. We all read from the same lurid script: the newspapers airbrush reality, then package it in a formula not much different from that of the men's magazines; the schools deny the joy in children's bodies, using desks to tie them down, boredom to torture them; businessmen screw us. Where do we find the high regard for human possibility so notoriously lacking in hard-core pornography? And where do I find the man or woman whose sexual imagination isn't a little haunted, too? So why this extra burden, this self-loathing, the exponential guilt? Who but me is booing me? And when I speak out, in my own defense, who but me is listening? It's a one-man show, on an empty stage — words, and more words — an act as lonely as sex with myself. I know the soliloquy as intimately as the woman spread out on the page or in my mind or in my bed — how hard it is to keep them apart! — yet no woman, no matter how hurt by this, has been less forgiving of me than I am of myself.

I can't remember why I looked inside my father's closet that first time. Maybe my father himself led me there, not consciously, of course, but simply by being who he was. His life led me there, to the dank of him, the jungle where his father had led *him* and told him to make it on his own, there beneath the leafy canopy that blocked out the light, there on the spongy ground crawling with unnamed fears, there with his big naked body he never loved, his dirty books and his dirty jokes, his domineering mother's dirty looks. He never made it out of the closet, out of the heat and stink of his mind. But with so much grief in there, he had to leave the door open just a crack. With so much confusion of jungle calls, he had to let out a little cry. Maybe I heard him.

Perhaps the only difference between us is that I've taken a step out of the closet. Denying my own wound has never gotten me anywhere except into deeper denials, which always creates suffering. Can you end suffering by legislating against it? Can you legislate against the past? Can you transcend it? For a while, I tried that, too — making God into a pinup, just one more unattainable object of desire.

It's said we're compelled to live out the unfulfilled dreams (and nightmares) of our parents. In this observation, there's no blame, but no easy assurance, either. My father, like most men of his generation, dreamt of women's bodies, not their souls, yet blushed if he talked in his sleep: the women weren't to know. He feared women, but they weren't to know that, either. He split himself down the middle: on one side was the responsible, hard-working family man; on the other was everything wild, and, because it was untrusted, seemingly savage. A deep wound separated the two worlds, and pornography was the balm he rubbed along it.

SELLING OUT

I'VE STARTED WEARING A TIE. To anyone who's known me for the past fifteen years, this is as improbable as if I'd started wearing a dress. I didn't even own a tie until recently, but I've been buying them at the thrift shop, for fifty cents each — modest, conservative ties. I'm not dressing as a clown. I'm trying to look like a businessman.

The first day I came to the office that way, there were some exaggerated double-takes, a couple of jokes, but no one seemed quite as surprised as I was. I went into the bathroom two or three times to check myself out in the mirror. Notwithstanding my beard (hardly a symbol of anything anymore) and my floppy curls, I looked respectable. I remembered to keep my shoes on, too, though for years I've worked barefoot; in the winter, I pad around the office in my socks.

Finally, I settled down to work. It was quiet, as it usually is. Once in a while a friend may stop in; every few months, a sub-scriber says hello. This day, of all days, there was a knock on the door: a couple from Georgia, wanting to meet the editor.

I got up to greet them. They were in their twenties, easygoing. He had long, blond hair and a generous smile. She was a little shy, standing off to the side. She wore a peasant dress. He wore a hippie shirt and overalls. I think they were barefoot, but I can't remember for sure. I was too worried about the way I was dressed. I wanted them to know this wasn't how I usually looked. I wanted them to know I was one of us — pure, poor, a prince of a guy in a pauper's disguise. But here I was, in my new disguise, already afraid it was working.

Why the tie? Oddly enough, it's because of a book I just read, Chogyam Trungpa's *Shambhala: The Sacred Path Of The Warrior*, a profound statement about learning who we really are, discovering our true power and dignity. To live as a spiritual warrior, Trungpa says, is to be always aware, the way a good fighter is aware. It means noticing every change — the rustling of branches, the rustling of thoughts. When the mind and body are synchronized, meditation isn't something we do (or don't do) once a day, but is instead a way of life.

A warrior pays attention to people, too. He gives up anything that is a barrier between himself and others. Trungpa respects tradition: the family, all the generations who came before us and advanced human life through hard work and sacrifice. The warrior honors the past as well as the present and does what is expected of him — not blindly, but with unerring sensitivity to the moment. There's nothing contradictory, Trungpa suggests, about living spiritually and wearing a three-piece suit to a business meeting. That is the appropriate attire, so why not wear it? To show others we're different, more original, perhaps smarter than they? This isn't the warrior's way. So, too, with how we stand, walk, sit. Feet belong on the floor, not on the desk, he says. It's too easy to put our feet on the desk. It suggests we're free, that our minds are free, but that kind of relaxation, Trungpa says, has nothing to do with real freedom.

To me, these were disquieting thoughts. I'd made a career out of being different, breaking the rules. Living authentically has meant, among other things, dressing to satisfy myself and not others, putting my feet where I pleased. Even though I ran a business, I never thought of myself as a businessman. I was a maverick publisher, in my heart a poet still, a seeker — not for success or profit, but for truth. Struggling to pay the bills enhanced the drama. Jeans and T-shirts, the more frayed the better, told the world who I was.

Trungpa's words came like a tap on the shoulder. I turned around and there it was, the obvious truth. Yes, I'm a poet, a romantic. And I'm also in business. I'm a businessman. My ambivalence about making money was hardly a sign of spirituality. Maybe dressing like a businessman would teach me something.

Wearing the tie makes me more aware than ever how deep-seated are my prejudices against wealth and success. Even the appearance of success makes me uncomfortable. Individually, I don't think I judge wealthy people more harshly than I do anyone else — but isn't that like the charitable racist who acknowledges there are some exceptions to the rule?

My way of seeing the world was shaped by the radical politics of the sixties. As a college student, I marched for civil rights. I wrote editorials against the Vietnam War. I pondered a world divided into haves and have-nots. Nothing seemed more important to me than to change this. When I got out of college, I became a newspaper reporter because I thought it would give me that chance.

Though my salary was modest and I lived in a small apartment in an unassuming neighborhood, I knew I had a great deal compared to the poor. I tried to make it obvious where my sympathies were. I grew a beard. I wore scuffed shoes. With a raised eyebrow and a wry smile, I got the point across: I was one of *us*, not one of *them*. But since, in New York City, the downtrodden and disenfranchised tended to be black and I tended to be white, there was always the possibility someone would misunderstand.

One summer night, my editor sent me to cover a race riot, cautioning me to stay behind police lines. I quickly discovered there were no police lines with snipers firing from a half-dozen rooftops. Well past midnight, I followed a couple of cops down a deserted street and then, somehow, lost them. I'd been up and down these streets before — indeed, this was the kind of neglected neighborhood I had pledged to turn into an urban paradise — but that was usually during the day, in the company of an anti-poverty worker or a black politician. They may or may not have been convinced I was one of *us*. Now, walking as quickly and quietly away from there as I could, I knew that from the superior vantage of a rooftop, there was no doubt: I was one of *them*.

I didn't get shot and I didn't save the world. That turned out to be more difficult than I'd imagined. The corporations and the government hadn't created the greed and the exploitation, I came to realize; rather, it was the greed in individuals, the confusion about how to live in the world, that created the oppressive institutions. That insight brought me to a crossroads: I could become cynical about humanity, with ample evidence that all our hells were self-created, or I could turn from the world to face myself, and see in my own habits of thought, my guilt and fear, the real enemy.

Starting *The Sun* was an opportunity to give form to this understanding, to marry working on myself with working in the world. But good causes are dangerous. They attract the right people for the right reasons; thus the traps are more subtle. Being devoted to truth is one thing; being devoted to an organization devoted to truth is something else. Ram Dass tells one of my favorite stories, about God and Satan walking down the street. The Lord bends down, picks something up, and gazes at it glowing radiantly in his hand. Curious, Satan asks what it is. "This," answers the Lord, "is truth." "Let me have that," says Satan, "I'll organize it for you."

I know how easy it is to lose the thread, to become so absorbed in the endless details, the organization of truth, that I forget why I'm here. How often have I pushed aside my own writing? How many days have I given of myself unstintingly — without pausing for a quiet moment, a really naked moment, a moment of truth? We can sell out overtly — doing something for the money rather than out of a deeply-felt need — or we can sell out by trading our reality for an identity, any identity. No role we play in this world is as big as who we really are.

My forgetfulness is at the heart of my dilemma about being a businessman. I become entangled in the role, enchanted. But it's like any other role — father, writer, lover. If I become too identified with it, I start feeling lost. My vision narrows: the world becomes shadowy, pale, a backdrop for the drama I'm enacting. Interestingly, the dramas all have one thing in common: fear. Not enough money, not enough love, not enough time. Instead of feeling creative and alive, I feel empty and powerless. Every struggle becomes a struggle for survival, as long as I'm wandering through this dream.

Into the dream, I bring my particular prejudices: my distrust of success, my conflicts about my own needs. These form the dream landscape in which I travel, like Don Quixote, mistaking my own projections for what's real. Here we have the noble poor — in my dream, all the poor are noble — and the undeserving rich. Once again, it's us versus them, a dream of separateness in which I'm endlessly divided from myself, from abundance, from true generosity of spirit.

How would the spiritual warrior avoid this trap? How would he pay the bills? How would he remember?

Before I go to bed at night, I pick out the tie I'll wear the next day. How long will I keep doing this? I don't know. For now, it helps me remember. I wake up in the morning and put on the tie and wake up a little more.

Some Enchanted Evening

My friend Ron is in California now, making movies or waiting tables. We never write and I don't know when I'll see him again. But I'll always remember something he once said, one of the most honest things I've ever heard a man say. "The only time I'm happy, really happy," Ron said, "is when I'm in a woman's arms."

I know, I know. . . . There are men about whom this isn't true at all, men for whom happiness is found only in another man's arms; men who are happy only when they're making money; men who are devoid of passion for anything or anyone, because their heartache is too great or because their hearts were never broken — yes, men to whom women are no more important than poetry to a rock. Or so it seems. Yet I wonder if this indifference isn't often a lie. There's a howling in all of us. Some admit it; others say it's the wind, and shut the window, and go to sleep; but in their dreams everything they touch screams.

What have I ever craved more than a woman's arms? To be up half the night, talking, laughing, making love — have I ever been closer to heaven? The bed becomes your church; you pass the collection plate back and forth until you've given too much, then your poverty becomes your gift. Your tears, her tears — I mean, when it's right, who can tell laughing from crying? And though, in days or months or years to come, you'll swear you were fooling yourself, you weren't; it really happened. In the midst of all that fluttering, between the spilled wine and the giggling and the breathless kiss, your hearts billowed out like great white sails, and above you for a moment hovered the dove.

For a long time, I disparaged romantic love, even as I yearned for it. Better, I said to myself, to long for true love, total selflessness without thought of return. Better to crave God's embrace than a woman's. What is romance, after all, but a golden chain that winds first around the heart, then around the neck? What sweeter lie do we whisper to ourselves than that another person can save us? The truth is they do, for a while — days or weeks or months, even years. But eventually we find that no one can save us from ourselves. The realization is stunning, like seeing a photograph of the earth taken from space. How mysteriously alone we are! How tempting to imagine that if we're loved, our loneliness will be dispelled.

Yet here I am, celebrating with champagne and flowers my second anniversary, with my third wife. My conceit, lustrous as her skin in the flickering candlelight, is that I've finally learned something about love. She's been married before, too. In the lines around her eyes, I trace the scars. But when she smiles, the pain is transfigured. I trust her pain, and what she's learned from it, and the light in her eyes — how can I not trust that? It's a beacon to me, a refuge. More than four walls can ever be, it's home. Am I a man in love, which is to say, as big a fool as God has made?

If I've learned anything, it's how little I've learned. Norma and I sip our champagne. A breeze from the window slaps the candle, and my memory calls up other nights, other eyes, other women I've lived with and loved. With each, I built a temple of hope, and placed upon the altar the unclaimed future, with the sunny side up. Our hands and tongues and lives wound around each other as effortlessly as morning light filling a room; you could no more separate us than take the blue from the sky. Yet here we are, in the long night of disbelief we were sure would never follow: we're together no more. With each, in turn, the tears became a rain, the rain became a river, and we rushed down the waters of life with no more control than a barrel.

In the movie *Last Tango in Paris*, there is a heart-rending scene that evokes, for me, the impenetrable mystery of loving someone: why two souls, different as sky and sea, are called from opposite ends of the universe to make together a home, a life.

Paul (played by Marlon Brando) discovers that his estranged wife has killed herself. Alone with her in the funeral parlor, he contemplates her lifeless body upon its bed of flowers, her face set in a smile that is nearly beatific — a death mask which betrays his memories of her as in life she betrayed him, as they betrayed each other, with bad decisions, indiscretions, broken vows. He curses her, vilely and furiously. It is shocking. We expect, foolishly, something different for the dead. And then, suddenly, he begins to cry, his hatred dissolving into grief, as time itself dissolves, and she is again his darling, his tender love, the one he reached for across the eons, and who reached for him, and then let go, and now has let go for good. "A man can live for two hundred years," he weeps, "and never understand his wife."

Is it the women I haven't understood, or myself? The need to love and be loved — how much of it really had to do with them, their individual temperaments, charms, braininess, magic, their faces so ordinary and so adored? What have I looked for in their eyes but a truer reflection of myself? How passionate I've been, in pursuit of life through these other lives. What a devotee of desire! Not merely for the honey breasts and milky thighs, not merely for tastes tasted, the stuttering tongue appeased — but desirous, most of all, for desire itself. I've been hungry for hunger. I've come before my women like a starving man to a banquet table laden with everything delicious and suddenly within reach, and sat there scowling, insisting that someone feed me, feed me with a smile, with her hair brushed back just so, with nothing else on her mind, with undying devotion to my hunger, my awful hunger. No one could do it right, at least not for long. And so we hurt each other, terribly — I, convinced I was starving; they, convinced my appetite was grotesque, for sex, for sorrow, for sympathy, but mostly for the party not to end. My need, finally, was to keep alive the possibility of deliverance. To give up the yearning for a woman to save me was terrifying, because it meant facing an ancient anguish I couldn't bear. To give up the promise of love — the dizzying romance that someone else could meet my needs, fill my emptiness, still the howling — would mean acknowledging just how profound my pain was. Better the bruised look, the turned back, the slammed door. Better the quixotic search for the next shapely savior. But, of course, it would happen again. We seek our completion in the strangest ways, but seek it we must. We reenact the old hurts, we summon forth the ghosts of Mom and Dad and resurrect for them a new body, a new face, a voice with just a hint of the old, and we bid them to sit down beside us, here at the banquet table, and beg them once again to feed us, please, and please, this time, with a little love.

But there are no love substitutes. There's love, and there's everything that masquerades as love, all those diamonds that turn out to be glass: the world's prizes, and the prizes of the flesh, and the prizes of the spirit, too, so that God became the one I turned to when the fairy tale sputtered and the night came on — God as Mom, God as Dad, a God as distant and unattainable as the painful memories I used God to mask. But did it really matter whom I knelt before? What I worshipped was my own longing; what I loved was what I was able to get.

My children sometimes play a game called "Opposites," in which everything you say is the opposite of what you mean; they are learning, as they grow older, that most of us speak that way all the time. Every time I've said, "I love you," hasn't it been a lie? What I loved was the way I felt when a woman talked to me, when I thought of her, when her sunlight slid across the big dark barn of my heart.

But this is like loving the postman because he brings you a letter you wrote to yourself a long time ago, in a time before time, when you were whole, and love was as natural as breathing, and you hadn't yet bought the lie that you needed someone else's approval to be complete, that enchantment resided in another's eyes, not yours. Deep within us that knowledge still throbs, in the heart that can't be broken, where the words *God* and *love* and *truth* are not distant signposts but closer than two bodies can ever be: closer than her hair, dark and storm-tossed the way I like it, splayed across my face; closer than her breath smelling of me, and mine of her, mingling above us; closer than her secret wish, whispered in my ear, for a finger here, and mine, for a tongue there; yes, closer than memory and regret. Closer than my mother a thousand miles above me, bending to pick me up; closer than my father at the door. Closer than close — where the tyranny we call "love" is seen for what it is: our human prison, for which we've fashioned the lock, and the key, and forever go on confusing the one with the other, and always in the name of love.

Have I learned a thing or two? Some humility about love is a start. I start with what is dead in me, what hungers for the kiss of life, what wants to live in astonishment — not *through* but *with* a woman — and I acknowledge how difficult this is. Did I say difficult, or impossible?

For example, I learn to leave my wife alone. For someone as unsure as I of his self-worth — longing for the kind word, the handout, the pressing of flesh on flesh — this is no small accomplishment, and often I fail. Then I get the chance not to blame her for my pain. There's her pain, too. Does she try to soothe it with a little lie? Do I, like a blind man, give her my hand to run across her hidden face, so I might know her darker features, her fear? Do I get angry, or do I forgive her? Do I love her, or write a poem about love gone astray?

I have a drawer full of poems — for my ex-wives; for the other women I've lived with; for women I've known briefly, and slept with once, or known no less intimately for never having touched them; for friends who, had we cared less for each other, might have been lovers, and lovers who cared enough to become friends. Knowing that my love is nine-tenths lie, I say I love them still: that they're here with me on this anniversary night as the men Norma has loved are with us, too; that if togetherness is mostly illusion so is separateness; and that all those we've loved, however imperfectly, have left their mark on us, and we on them.

I fasted for a week before our wedding day, to purify myself, but by the time the ceremony started I was more dizzy than pure. I promised Norma the sweet air of me, but knew I'd deliver the meat. No angel touched me as I nervously recited the vows — which, two years later, seem both practical and preposterous. You need volumes to get you through the hard times, or nothing so much as silence.

We lift our glasses and gaze at each other romantically, before one of us breaks the spell with a wink. We both know what an absurd yet touching drama this is: this marriage rooted in human frailty and conceit but rooted, too, in God's will. Yes, we know — until the next awful moment when we forget, and have to struggle against the amnesia drawn before us like the darkest of curtains. Then grief becomes our bond. Grief, joy — one turns to the other quicker than you can say, "How was your day?"

And who's to say which is more love's measure? I didn't know I'd fallen in love with Norma until the first time I saw her cry. I'm falling still: through our shared loneliness, gathered into our hearts like a wild bouquet, then hurled away; through the sounds our bodies make, rolling together like chords; through echoes of plea-sure. One moment we're "in," the next moment we're "out" of love. We agree, over the flickering candlelight, that we can scarcely say which serves us better.

THE WRITING ON THE WALL

It STARTED WITH A LINE from the writings of Norman O. Brown: "Everything is only a metaphor; there is only poetry." This seemed to say it all. This was the reminder I wanted on my wall.

I don't remember what I put up next. Probably the quotation from Ram Dass: "I do crummy things. I do beautiful things. Does that mean I'm good or I'm evil? I'm neither. I just am." Or the picture of my children. Soon, there were those wonderful lines from Tagore. And Auden. And Rilke. And Kerouac's instructions to writers: "Accept loss forever. . . . No fear or shame in the dignity of your experience." And the extraordinary portrait of John Lennon, taken just days before he was killed, his eyes seemingly dark with the secret, the last surprise life was waiting to spring.

The words and pictures edged to the left and to the right, like a city pushing into the countryside, and up toward the ceiling and down toward the floor, until the cracked plaster and peeling paint were almost entirely paved over. "Sy's wall," my friends called it. Occasionally, one of them would step around my desk for a better look. After all, this was the graffiti of my inner life. If you knew what to look for, you'd see whole histories reflected. In the lament of my landlord: "You can't pay your bills and you're happy. I pay mine and I'm miserable. I don't know — who's got the better life?" In E.B. White's description of *New Yorker* editor Harold Ross's simple dream: "It was pure and had no frills. He wanted the magazine to be good, to be funny, to be fair," and in pursuit of this vision, he "spent himself recklessly on each succeeding issue, and with unabating discontent." In Thomas Crowe's haunting summons: "I am through with my love of suffering and the words that describe that love." And there were my pinups: Gandhi and Thomas Merton and that old Indian saint, Neem Karoli, who peered at me from beneath bushy eyebrows, his loving scowl skeptical of everything I advertised as love, these inspirations, this wall of longings, this wailing wall — for isn't what we strive for precisely what we think we lack?

Ironically, I rarely looked at what I'd put up. For the most part, as soon as I came across something worth remembering and tacked it up, the thrill of discovery began to wane, the moment of revelation became a memory, the unfamiliar phrase became one more familiar thing on the wall, taken as much for granted as the birds and the traffic outside, the sunlight slanting through the blinds. To take life for granted is natural and regrettable, which is why we put up reminders not to take life for granted, then ignore them.

Last Christmas, we painted the office for the first time in years, and I had to take everything off my wall. I didn't want to do it, because I knew it would force me to consider each quotation and picture, and decide which ones I wanted to keep. I put it off until the very last night, when I had to roll up the rug and move the furniture into the hall. Alone in my office, in the empty room that echoed me back to myself, my hands undid what my hands had done. But how was I to judge which things were worth saving? That photograph of me and Ram Dass on my front porch: all I saw in it now was my mugging for the camera, posing with the president, confusing celebrity-fucking with love. No, no, I tell myself, that's too harsh: it's because of what Ram Dass taught me about love that I cherish him, not because he's a celebrity. But is that true? How utterly untrustworthy I am when it comes to love. The word itself is a whore, bedding down for the night with whoever will pay. It's the way we're built, with these minds willing to betray the heart's greatest sacrifice for a little smile, a little cash. Or have you never heard yourself trading on the best of what you've done, imagining that you were only drawing on the interest, and leaving the balance of yourself intact? Isn't Ram Dass himself so endearing because he's honest about his pride, his lusts, the fast deals he made in the corridors of spiritual power? What's wrong with keeping his smile before me?

Or the smile of Patricia Sun, she of the perfect teachings and perfect teeth: how much better blondes look in the Light! She's up there to remind me about forgiveness, but can I forgive myself the reminder she's sexy, too, which makes what she says a bit more compelling?

On through the night, photograph by photograph, quotation by quotation, my wall came down; memories came undone. Like the mind uncoiling from itself as it drifts to sleep, the images on my wall one by one trailed away and disappeared, leaving behind what was always there: cracked plaster, peeling paint. Oddly, I no longer found the emptiness menacing. None of the teachers, none of the teachings, made quite as much sense anymore as their absence did. Nearly a year later, my wall is still bare. In a sense, I've replaced fifty different reminders with one.

But how hard it is — how much more subtle than what I do or don't put on a wall, or say to a friend, or write in a magazine — to make my own way, free of spiritual conceit. No wonder my harshest judgment falls on those I imagine to be even more conceited than I. My compassion fans out in loving waves to the deluded racist, the mass murderer, the bum who lies to my face. But for the new-age con artist or the zealous devotee of a phony guru, I have nothing but ridicule, and for the so-called master himself, contempt.

A couple of years ago, it was reported that Swami Muktananda, one of the most respected meditation masters to have come to America from India, and an avowed celibate, had been having sex regularly with his teenaged disciples, and threatening with bodily harm anyone who complained about it — as well as amassing a small personal fortune in a Swiss account. About the same time, Richard Baker, one of the foremost Zen Buddhist teachers in America, became embroiled in a scandal about his sexual conduct. More recently, Bhagwan Shree Rajneesh, the Indian sage who owns thirty Rolls Royces, ended a four-year silence; in his first speech, he denounced his chief spokeswoman and other top followers in a controversy involving charges of murder and blackmail.

Muktananda and Baker and Rajneesh were wise men, knowledgeable about the nature of reality. I don't question that they've been places I haven't; to deny that would be as foolish as insisting that some exotic island halfway around the world, which I'd never seen and wasn't likely to, for that reason didn't exist. Some people devote their lives to becoming wealthy, and end up multi-millionaires; others devote their lives to spiritual study, and end up rich in understanding. There's nothing particularly mysterious about it: spiritual laws, enshrouded in secrecy, are secrets only until you figure them out.

To seek truth so earnestly that nothing else matters — neither sex nor money nor status — is hard for most of us to imagine. Yet the biographies of the great teachers suggest great sacrifice and are offered as inspiration to the rest of us, who hear the summons but stand silently by the window, watching our destiny like a great dark cloud rush by. Driven by the winds of compromise and practicality, we assure ourselves that traveling to work in the morning is a kind of meditation, and that a simpler life would be better, but there are these bills. And this ache each night, this ache we've learned isn't for a lover or a snack or a pill — what else is there? What are we aching for? And one day we find ourselves staring at the words of a Muktananda or a Rajneesh, and we are reminded of what else there is. The arrow of our longing flies straight to its target, reminding us, as it hits, that the heart longs only for God.

The deceit of the guru — that his nut-brown hands raised heavenward in the morning are at night undoing a fifteen-year-old's bra — is somehow harder to stomach than the lies of a politician (who, after all, promises only heaven on earth), or the more forgivable trespasses of a wife or a friend, because we know their love is haunted, as ours is, as everyone's is. Even, it turns out, the love of these lovers of God, these sinners in drag as saints. It's all one can do to keep from closing the door not just on fake saints but on the very idea of saintliness; not just on bargain-basement godliness but on God, too.

Still, I knew that my anger toward people like Muktananda was keeping me from understanding something important. It wasn't until I got a letter from a friend who had followed and then disavowed Muktananda that I realized what it was.

In his letter, Marc referred to the days before Muktananda came to America, to a younger man who did not want to be drawn into the world, did not want disciples, told everyone he was a renunciate and a loner. More and more people came to him anyway.

Marc suggested that Muktananda had, in fact, attained great spiritual power and "had wisely been afraid of being tempted by the world, by wealth and sex and emulation," and "had ultimately fallen to the lowest in himself just as he had feared, giving and giving until there was nothing left to give. What terror he must have endured. I feel he is probably deserving of our pity and compassion."

It was so obvious a conclusion, yet revelatory for me. Instead of reacting to Muktananda and other fallen heroes as if their arrogance and dishonesty were a personal insult to me, as if — simply because they set themselves up as saints — I had every right to expect saintliness from them, I could instead remember that they were as deserving of forgiveness as anyone, that if their power was greater so were their imperfections. Who can say what dark angels they wrestled with?

What a golden opportunity America presents to these Eastern holy men to succumb to the temptations of fame and wealth. For surely this society, materialistically magnificent, is a mirror to the spiritually rich East. Having mastered the inner realms, these would-be saints get the chance to endure the American stations of the cross: instant celebrity, computerized miracles, California girls. Our affluence is as exquisite a challenge for them as a suffocatingly hot hotel room in Benares would be for a businessman from Milwaukee setting off to find his guru.

Of course, it may be that we only hear about one type of teacher. Back in the sixties, the more successful communes knew better than to give themselves a name, and I suspect that a similar wisdom may prevail among God's truest servants.

Again and again, I'm struck by the consequences of mythologizing someone else's power, whether a guru or a beautiful stranger. To respect people is one thing; to raise them up on a pedestal merely shows how deep a hole I've dug for myself. Making myself lower than another isn't a sign of humility; rather, it's an insidious kind of pride, in which I bow before my real or imagined weaknesses, making them the sum of me. True humility lies in forgiving myself for being so perplexingly human, and forgiving others for pretending they're any less human than I.

HAND IN HAND

AT THE BEACH, there's garbage everywhere, washed up by the hurricane: metal cans, plastic milk jugs, rotten wood. A dead turtle, the largest I've ever seen, lies at the water's edge. As we step around it, I feel a ripple of revulsion. I know death is natural, like breathing, like the tides, but I'm uncomfortable around it anyway, as if it were somehow . . . wrong.

Hand in hand, we walk along, past fishermen, a few families. Most of the houses are boarded up for winter; no one is in the water on this sunny, chilly day. I've never figured out why I'm drawn to the ocean this time of year. I grow somber, melancholy. I brood about Important Things. I scan the horizon, as if the answers were out there, coming toward me on the next wave — so that if I stood long enough, and squinted hard enough with my collar turned up and the wind in my face, I'd learn something new, but it seldom happens that way.

Nor do I find answers when I gaze into Norma's eyes, scanning the horizon where her world meets mine. I want to make sure there are no dark clouds, no mistakes I made a minute ago or an hour ago that have churned up a storm, but looking for safety I never find any.

Answers, safety. Surely, the sea is laughing, as we walk along the murmuring shore. Surely, there is mockery in the rising wind. We've come here to remind ourselves of what life seems intent on making us forget — those truths that run through the hands like sand. We've come to retrace the changing shoreline of our love, and rebuild what the busy days will wash away again. We've come, for a few days, to cut a deal with eternity: to talk without looking at the clock; to cheat boredom and jealousy and worry with the intensity of being together; to go beyond where the waves break in our hearts, to where it's calm instead of fearful, and bring that feeling back with us — if the sea, murmuring and mocking, will let us.

We call these days a vacation, as if this time were somehow less important or less demanding than time spent at our desks. We might as well say the busyness of our daily lives is a vacation from facing ourselves. How much easier it is to keep oiling the moving parts than to question where we're going. How seductive is the illusion of higher purpose. Norma, learning to be a doctor, often neglects her own health. I, blessed with work that engages me so fully I don't even think of myself as having a job, know that without a task in front of me, I'm lost. I pace the rooms of my mind. I notice things that I overlook when I'm busy: the mismatched pieces of my personality; the sags and wrinkles and broken springs; the self-portraits on the wall that still don't look quite right. Maybe if I rearranged them.

How much more tempting it is to get back to my desk than to endure myself. How foolish it seems to waste time on the unanswerable questions when there's so much unanswered mail.

There is, too, our home in the country with its no-nonsense demands: wood for the winter; pipes that freeze. Norma calls to remind me to bring home coffee, toilet paper. Surely, I don't wish to forget anything: the mail, the wood, my morning run, lunch with a friend. . . . Of course, the list is endless, for we aren't responsible only to ourselves. There's the need to clean up the air and the water and the cities, to eliminate poverty, to end war. Coffee and toilet paper. Life doesn't let up. But we do, little by little, pretending our inner lives are a weight our bodies have been burdened with, that love is something we make for a few minutes at the end of the day.

We pursue the goal of world peace as if it were something to achieve, through peace talks or peace marches. Even lovers, eyeing each other across the kitchen table, confuse real change with simply talking about it — then back away from each other, defeated. We circle our feelings, as if they were snakes in a pit. How can Reagan, who so denies his own deep grief, contemplate the grief of the Russian people, so devastated in the past by war? How can the Russians, ruled by a government that regiments their lives like an unforgiving father, contemplate the American version of freedom with anything but incredulity and a little fear? Who is brave enough to turn from the enemy to face the more formidable enemy within?

I regard, with an upraised eye, the rooms of the heart I share with Norma. How chaotic they can seem; how squalid and dark, with their heavy furniture we've brought from our pasts. There's the wish to redo things, replace all the hand-me-downs with something contemporary and bright, bring in the ferns. Yet isn't it precisely our different styles, the patterns we never dreamed would work together — and in hurt and angry moments, insist never will — that give us a chance to learn something only we can teach each other?

Not long before our trip, I sat beside her, dark and unhappy. Between us was an unforgiving desert neither of us knew how to cross. I was jealous — although that doesn't seem like the right word, since my rival was no one in particular but other men in general. My real rival was an unreasoning fear of other people's attractiveness. Yet that wasn't it either. What I felt was the long shadow of the big fear behind all my fears, the fear that mocks me as unlovable, and apologizes for my existence, and whispers cunningly that the woman beside me is the only one I can trust, and that I can't trust her . . . that she is my salvation, and my ruin . . . the one to love, and the one to fear.

I'd been stranded in this barren place enough times to know that talking about it wouldn't help. Insights about ourselves are useful — until they become enshrined as psychological truth, and are called forth like a benediction over every troublesome scene, having ironically become yet another excuse not to feel. But an excuse not to feel was precisely what I was after. So I talked and Norma listened and Norma talked and I listened and the conversation moved through the night and the next night and the next like a new highway twisting and turning across the map of our lives, a road nobody asked for but here it was, tearing up our moments of silence and repose the way a bulldozer snaps trees.

After a week of this, we went to a movie. Perhaps *Kiss Of The Spider Woman*, the story of a friendship between two prisoners, speaks no more eloquently than many other films about the search for love, but when we left the theater, I wept — for Luis and Valentin's broken lives, and for the sadness in all of us. Each wave of sorrow carried into shore yet more wreckage from the past week, and soon I was crying for the old shipwreck of my childhood — a far different experience than talking about it, as great as the difference between water and the letters that spell it.

The price I pay for avoiding grief is to make it a stranger, feared and powerful. But when I let all my sorrows gather and I mourn openly, then grief is grief, uncomplicated by fear or the need for sympathy. Ironically, I feel strongest in these moments — not invincible, but not threatened, either. I stop blaming Norma, or anyone else, for my pain. This is peace as I know it.

How wonderful, writes Pablo Neruda, that a man and a woman, "after many travels, and with much deliberation, accomplish a great novelty — they share one bed. . . . What dues we pay on this planet, for loving one another in peace."

By the time we get to the beach, our personal storm has spent itself, as has the hurricane. The small resort town seems more muted than usual — roof shingles torn off and scattered, broken signs hanging from one hinge — and so are we. But it's good to be reminded of the power of the sea, and to breathe the air that follows a storm.

BABY FAT

MY OLDEST DAUGHTER, MARA, makes me a big pan of it every Christmas. She knows I like anything she makes — like most parents, I'm shamelessly sentimental — but my delight over the fudge is especially keen. It doesn't matter that this year it's no surprise. In years past, we'd conspire to create some mystery until it was time to open gifts, but this Christmas, when I pick up Mara and Sara at their mother's house for our holiday visit, the secret's out. She's made two pans this year, and they're too big to hide. Besides, she's nearly eleven, too old to be excited by her Dad's feigned surprise. Standing by the car, she hands me the aluminum foil-wrapped pans to put beside her suitcase. She shrugs and says, "This is the fudge." Then she glances at me uncertainly and sighs. "Is it OK I told you?"

The fudge is, properly, "Elyse's Super Fudge." My sister Elyse created it and passed the recipe along. It's hard to believe there's not a spoonful of sugar or a sliver of chocolate in it. Fifteen years ago, when sugar had risen to the top of my list of *don'ts*, my sister, with a good-natured wink, handed me my first slice. It looked so rich and dark; she assured me it would make my sweet tooth quiver while leaving my conscience at peace. "You're kidding," I said, turning it over as suspiciously as a rabbi inspecting his salad for bacon bits. Refusing to eat sugar — an austerity which, for me, was just this side of giving up sex — was only my latest and most fanatical attempt to stave off that old and unrelenting foe: my appetite.

It hasn't always been this way. According to family legend, improbable though it seems, at one time I wouldn't eat at all. I was a "bad eater," they said — so bad it took two of them, my mother and my grandmother, to convince me to open my tiny mouth and swallow. One would push me on my toy horse, the other would follow with poised spoon. If my father happened to be at home, he'd help out, too. "Take a bite for President Truman," he'd croon. "Take a bite for Joe DiMaggio."

What dedication! What imagination! What patience! Of the latter, though, I can only guess, as they never included in their reminiscences the inevitable disappointments and failures, the food I must have spit back at them, the anger, the napkin run across my lips. . . . How old could I have been? Probably, I was at the age when children learn to say *no*. How perplexing this is for parents. Yet what an appropriate response *no* is for most things we're asked to do in this world. Still, I had to eat. What point was there in developing normally — in building a strong ego and mature sense of identity — if I proceeded, spitefully, to waste away?

In their minds they were, I suppose, being kind. They were all overweight — my father extravagantly so — and associated food with well-being and security and love. Still, when I look back at the photographs taken of me then, I don't understand their alarm. A bad eater, you'd think, might look a little scrawny or frail, but there's no hint of boniness, nothing gaunt in that chubby-faced smile. The baby fat never melted away: my tummy kept getting rounder; my plump arms were the kind grownups love to squeeze. When I was eight, the doctor put me on a diet to lose twenty pounds — a rite of passage which made me fully a part of the family, in which everyone was either dieting or pretending to.

I lost the twenty pounds. For years afterward, my parents praised me for my "willpower" during those few months, though my restraint had more to do with shame. Anyway, I promptly put the weight back on; in my school pictures, I'm one of the biggest kids in the class. Since I was, thankfully, tall and big-boned, I was never as grotesquely fat as the *really* fat kids, a terribly important distinction at the time.

Forty years later, a grown man with children of my own, I'm still struggling with my appetite. Like my parents, and their parents before them, I've made food into a symbol. Eating has become a way to satisfy needs that have nothing to do with food — which is, of course, impossible. As impossible, for me, as taking just one bite. As impossible as the feeling I'm reaching for when I reach for something sweet, for the brief joy, the flowering happiness I can never really reach. So I reach again.

My daughter's fudge, this generous gift, this gift of love meant to last for days — I wonder, will it last an hour? Will I reach for it, as I've always done, as if I'm reaching into the past? Will I keep on eating, even after the sweetness cloys? Why haven't I ever been able to eat just one piece without eating the whole pan?

I have a friend who, like me, used to be a fat kid and, like me, has struggled ever since to keep from being a fat adult. One day we were talking about our eating habits, the way two generals might discuss the strategies they'd used in the same intractable war. I asked if he ate any snacks after dinner. "No," he said. "Don't you get hungry?" I wanted to know. He smiled ruefully. "I've been hungry all my life."

Was my friend being melodramatic? When I told him I knew exactly what he meant, was I? Here we were, two good-looking guys, healthy, well-built. But looks, like nearly everything else, deceive. I don't know anyone who isn't hungry — for food, or power, or security, or romance. Only our winding scars are different.

At 175 pounds, I could stand to lose some weight, but I'm six feet tall and run or exercise nearly every day. I'm not fat in the eyes of the world. Still, I think of myself that way.

I crave food the most when I'm hurt or bored or lonely and don't want to acknowledge it, like an ideologue dismissing facts because they get in his way. The more I lie, the hungrier I get. How odd, for the heart to be buttressed against its own sorrows, a fortress built of tears I might have wept. How odd, these endless diets and ridiculous struggles and jail-house rules meant to save me. Instead of real hunger — self-regulating, responsive to the moment, as subtle as the body's other whisperings — there's this beast, howling to be fed.

I've weighed a few pounds less than I do now, and I've weighed more — nearly fifty pounds more, when I was an unhappy graduate student. But no matter how much I've weighed, no matter how many push-ups and sit-ups I've done, no matter how many calories I've counted and miles I've run, I've never liked my body. Even today, when I'm in better shape than ever, I feel guilty about the way I look.

I've known women who have reviled themselves for not resembling *Playboy* bunnies. Just so perversely have I regarded myself in the mirror, always falling short of my imaginary ideal — as if only my head were me and everything below it an accident, some other guy's body, a mistake.

I know that seeing myself this way is wrong. My body reflects back to me the exact shape of my thoughts and feelings, so that the image I see in the mirror is itself a mirror, an uncanny reflection, in flesh, of all my joys and longings, all the things I've accepted or fled from. The extra pounds merely tell me how much protection from myself I've thought I needed. They're insulation from the pain of living — hardly a mistake. The only mistake is hating myself for still believing I need protection, for condemning the part of me who's still terrified of emptiness and scrambles back from the abyss, wanting to be fed.

I've never been able to write about feeling fat. Being at the type-writer is difficult for me on the best of days, and this subject is too painful. I'd wind up in front of the refrigerator instead.

But this year, I surprised myself during Christmas. I didn't sit down with my daughter's gift and eat both pans. I showed some moderation. I didn't make something as innocent as eating fudge into a sin. For me, that's a miracle. How long we stand knocking at the door to ourselves, hoarse from calling our name out, before the door opens, and we let ourselves in.

Heartened by my seeming progress, I thought I'd give the writing a try. But one memory leads to another, a pain that's deep leads to one deeper still. Yesterday, I panicked. Here I was, summoning ghosts — and the ghosts arrived! My triumph over a pan of fudge suddenly seemed pathetic.

It was a bad moment. I wanted to run from the typewriter, from myself, from the scorn and failure of having been a fat kid. But I wanted, too, to take a step closer, to hang over the edge. I wanted to reach for the smiling, chubby boy in the photograph, to reach across the years and draw him near, to hold him and tell him about the hunger, tell him that we eat and eat and eat but the hunger never disappears.

BETWEEN THE LINES

H E WAS ON HIS WAY TO WORK, my friend said, and had stopped for gas. That's when he noticed her. She was walking along the street, the sunlight streaming behind her, too far away at first for him to see her face. But something about her attracted him — the way she walked, perhaps, some swirl of color and motion, the signature her body made with hands and breath and hair. He gazed at her, longingly, furtively, with that look that comes over a man, that look so hopeful and so wretched.

My friend paused and smiled at me wryly.

"Then she got closer and I could see who she was," he said, with the resigned tone of someone who'd been the butt of a bad joke. In an instant, his longing turned sour: old memories of struggle and blame overwhelmed him, driving away whatever desire he'd momentarily felt for this beautiful, too-familiar stranger, this woman who'd once been his wife.

I laughed, though I knew that to him it was dark humor. I'd rarely heard him say a kind word about his ex-wife. Intellectually, he knew better than to blame her; emotionally, he was still bruised, and thus on the defensive — with less-than-tender references to her when he was in my company and a seemingly unfeeling silence when he was in hers. To be so attracted to her, even momentarily, made him feel vulnerable, as if his defenses had been breached — and they had. Looking at an attractive stranger, aren't we also looking at what's incomplete in us, for some angle of beauty where we feel broken, some tenderness where we've forgotten how to love ourselves?

That same week, I was trying to decide whether to accept a personals ad for *The Sun*.

The ad was from a "shapely, long-haired, dark-eyed beauty" looking for a "slim, handsome SM (20-45) magical playmate with heart of gold and free spirit to soar with, unfold with, bake bread, travel to South Seas." It had been sitting on my desk for a couple of months, staring at me reproachfully. I'd promised to let the woman know if I was going to use it, but I couldn't make up my mind.

My dilemma had to do not only with this particular ad but with personals in general. Did I want them in *The Sun*? Did they serve a useful purpose? Could anything be wrong with hearts reaching out this way?

Or did such advertising serve our worst fears? Did it speak to one kind of loneliness — the loneliness of people separated from each other — by ignoring the deeper loneliness of people separated from themselves? I wondered, with two divorces behind me, if I was the right person to decide. I had spent, it seemed, half my life foolishly seeking the heights of love and the other half falling ruinously from them.

I kept studying the ad, trying to figure out what disturbed me about it. Like most personals, it seemed a little sad, a brave and foolish attempt to present oneself as flawless, as if describing a car, not a person. We so rarely advertise what's best in us — our doubts, our contradictions. The ad, too, struck me as hopelessly wistful in its yearning for a man with no responsibilities but with infinite compassion. It was as if a heart of gold were like a perfect nose or curly hair, something you were or weren't born with, instead of something earned by taking on such responsibilities as life asks. We all have responsibilities — if not to a spouse or to children, then to a job, a friend, the life of a community, the garden we planted that's now overgrown with weeds. Only in the context of our responsibilities, our rootedness in time and place, does our freedom mean anything. To soar is wonderful, but even balloons have strings.

"And what about men who aren't slim?" Catherine, our office manager, protested. It's one thing, she said, to reach out to a kindred soul; it's another thing to be so choosy about the body that soul arrives in. Guiltily (I prefer slim women), I agreed. We've all made slaves of ourselves — women especially — because of someone else's idea of beauty: we hide what's shattered in ourselves behind the plaster cast of beauty that won't fit, that never fit.

And yet, we each have preferences; it's as shameful to deny them as to insist that another person conform. Couldn't I remember that personals are pleas for help, harmless in themselves, clumsy expressions of genuine feeling? We all get lonely. Some feel it in the depths of their soul, and never speak of it; others feel it like a knife in the groin or a dull throb in the heart. Hands reach out for other hands. Something in us wants to blossom, but remains dark, unborn. Haven't we all dreamt of the perfect stranger? Haven't we looked into other eyes, hoping to see a perfect reflection of ourselves, or, better yet, a reflection of our perfect selves, our wholeness, which we've denied and veiled? Believing ourselves incomplete, we seek completion. How many times, with how many strangers, have we found it? Oh, the joy of thinking we've found it! The loneliness that runs in us, endless as a spring flood, turns into a moonlit river; stars come out of a darkened sky. Overnight, we become glorious. The stunted parts of ourselves are forgotten; sorrow seems to pass like a season, one that can never return. . . . But return it does, as surely as rain falls to earth, and lovers become strangers once again. That depthless moment, when we looked into each other's eyes, that unbelievable moment when there was no "you" or "I" — where did it go? Were we only dreaming? Was love a lie?

Love is no lie but we lie endlessly about it. We lie to each other because we lie to ourselves. We're in too much pain to see our fantasies for what they are — futile attempts to compensate for the ways in which we're wounded. We look for someone whose looks and personality, joys and heartaches, discoveries and denials somehow "balance" our own.

Let me tell you, I've looked as fervently, embraced as passionately, made love as wildly as any man might — any man whose sorrows were my sorrows, who worshipped at the same temples during the same endless night. My loneliness called me to my hour of prayer at the altar of someone not myself — someone who, pray God, needed me, too. How tempting, then, to advertise myself not as supplicant but as savior. To make it convincing, I needed to convince not just her but myself. Which of us was more likely to second-guess my most generous gestures, conceived in the hour when the only kindness I sought was not to be left alone? Would I proclaim my great love then, or my great need, or some artful arrangement of the two, like a flower with its thorns? Perhaps she'd want the bouquet anyway. Honesty was advertised, in all honesty. But what was the truth?

I'm still a dreamer who sleeps fitfully. I wake up for a while, then fall back into my dream. In it, my wife is the perfect stranger. When she disappoints me, when I doubt her perfect love — or when I fear she's doubting mine — the dream shimmers. In the dream, it seems as if love has died. In fact, all that's died is one more illusion.

I realize that these aren't universal sentiments, that many people approach this subject more playfully. They look at the nighttime sky and see the man in the moon, not dark craters. If romance is an illusion, they might say, so is everything. There's pathos in that story about my friend's ex-wife, but there's also joyful absurdity. There's artifice in the personals, but there's an element of theater, too; they're *meant* to excite and allure.

The message in this ad seemed to be: the fantasy in me seeks the fantasy in you. The pain in that yearning may not be obvious to everyone, but it is to me. It's buried beneath years of pretending, hard to see. In a way, it's like the columns of personals. They're buried in the back of the paper, with their opaque meanings, their cryptic abbreviations. In these strange times, these times of anonymity and grinding isolation, is this how we're meant to find each other — in the small type, not reading between the lines?

I DIDN'T NEED another typewriter when Jeffrey gave me the Underwood about ten years ago. I still had my old portable, which had served me dutifully since college, a sleek and sturdy Olympia on which I'd typed my way through graduate school, my first newspaper job, Europe, and two marriages. Still, I figured it wouldn't hurt to have another typewriter around the office, though I suspected I'd be the only one who would use it. My preference for old-fashioned manuals was looked on, even then, as embarrassingly romantic and impractical, and as further evidence, if any was needed, that I wasn't happy unless I was struggling, typing and retyping the same sentences; pounding the words into place; needing no help from electricity, thank you — the persistent hum of an electric unnerving me, as if the typewriter itself were waiting impatiently for the next word.

As it turned out, Jeffrey's timing was uncanny. For later that spring, on a brilliant afternoon — the doors and windows open to the fragrant breeze and the birds and the low rumble of traffic from Rosemary Street — I stood by the open door, watching my old Olympia sail past me. It hit the grassy strip near the parking lot, the carriage extended like a climber's broken leg after a fall. A few more feet and it would have smashed on the asphalt, which was, no doubt, my enraged lover's intention when she hurled it out the door.

Why were we fighting? It's odd that I don't remember. If I could remember — if, remembering the honeyed sunlight that day, and the blossoms dotting the branches outside, I could also remember the passion and skill we brought to our arguing; if I could remember how, when we made love, we clutched at each other as later we would clutch at straws — why, then I might understand what comes between two people and tears them apart, the way ice with a long moan breaks from the river, the way love's broken vows break the heart.

But memory, like love, fails. I remember the thud. The carriage bell rang once with the impact; then again, as if in disbelief. The

Olympia worked after that, but not well, the way a car that's been in a wreck is never the same — and who knows why? Our machines may be more a part of us than we imagine, as intimate a reflection of our longings and losses as our own face in the glass.

Thus, the Underwood replaced the Olympia on my desk and, before long, in my heart. I didn't care much for its looks — big and boxy, a lusterless battleship gray — but it worked flawlessly. It was, after all, built not to please the eye but to last, to endure changes in fashion and technology, to stand up to a lifetime of use, to outlast whoever had bought it, as it probably had.

I knew that Jeffrey hadn't owned it long. I wondered who had brought it home, spanking new, some fifty years before, and set it proudly on the table, and called the family in for a look. I wondered how many other people had owned it over the years. How many nights had someone switched on a small lamp and rolled a sheet of paper into the carriage and waited — a cup of coffee nearby, cigarette smoke drifting to the ceiling — waited in suspended time for the right words to come, waited under that pale yellow light for the image that rises from within, that joins what is seen with what is hidden, that makes the world anew. How patiently he waited — no wires, no batteries, no blinking cursors urging him on. For every second our modern conveniences save us, they remind us as well of the time we've lost. "Time is always running out for machines," Wendell Berry observed. "They shorten our work by simplifying it and speeding it up, but our work perishes quickly in them, too, as they wear out and are discarded."

Berry was reflecting on agriculture, not writing. But writing is a physical act as well. What I write *with* affects what I write. The difference may be subtle, but no more so than the choice of words, the rhythm, the silence between the noisy pounding of the keys. I know of a poet, accustomed to composing on yellow lined legal pads, who ran out of his favorite kind of paper at a writers' conference; he couldn't write another word.

Using the Underwood every day became a habit, like the way I wash the dishes or answer the phone — shaping me, defining me, making my life more mine. Just as the details of a painting make its subject unique and recognizable, so do our habits — good habits and bad and everything in between — give our lives their weight, their texture, their light and dark. No one sits down and writes. You sit down somewhere, in a certain chair. You write with a pencil — always a pencil — or a cheap Bic, or an expensive fountain pen. If you're me, you write on a typewriter that, no matter how demanding I am, never protests, any more than Gibraltar protests the swirling waters; a typewriter that endures, patiently and silently, the endless rewriting, that receives me like the perfect friend who listens without judgment, letting me lie, letting me change my story, letting me reveal myself.

Am I describing a love affair with something inanimate — with gears and levers, with cold, gray steel? Or am I extolling me, the qualities in me the Underwood symbolizes: patience, durability, strength? It's hard to separate us. Why try? My piano is inanimate, too — but when I touch it, it touches me. Do I distinguish the longing that music awakens in me from the music itself? What's inanimate, anyway, except that which lives just beyond our touch? How alive this dead world is when we love it!

On the gray keys flecked with white-out, I see my errors and confusions covered over, forgiven, pure now as snow. In the stolid, forgettable design, I see a mystery — steel bent to the service of language, "lifeless" atoms waiting on human thought. In its sturdiness, its seeming indestructibility, I see the pact I make with the future, hoping that I, too — with my words, my deeds — have built something to last.

One day last month, I was absorbed in my writing, the Underwood familiar and unnoticed beneath my hands. How dreamlike, how transparent the world becomes — the desk, the chair, the room, all unnoticed — as I look for that other, inner world, searching the darkness like the moon sliding across the sky.

Word by word, I raised up sentences; word by word, I brought them down. I wrote and rewrote, typed and retyped — the keys dancing beneath me — until I heard an unfamiliar sound. I hit the next key, but nothing happened. Something had broken. My Underwood, my heart.

The typewriter had been in the shop before, for minor repairs. This time, I was told, it couldn't be fixed. The necessary part wasn't available; no one stocked it; no one in America even made manual typewriters anymore.

Isn't there anything you can do? I implored. Like a doctor accustomed to dealing with the desperately ill, the repairman smiled kindly. Not really, he said. Nothing? I persisted. He shrugged. Well, he said, if we could find another Underwood as old as yours, we might salvage the part from it. He gestured toward another typewriter whose owner was praying for a similar miracle. How long had he been waiting? I asked. He smiled again. About two years.

I brought my typewriter back to the office. I couldn't bear to throw it away but I was unwilling to search high and low for its twin. I believed in miracles; I also believed in my endless capacity for fooling myself, for denying my losses. This isn't the world of words, I reminded myself, where anything can be fixed; time has the last word here.

I bought another typewriter, one of those fancy electronic ones, and used it a few days. It was a great machine; the typing was effortless, as effortless as I'd like my writing to be — my feelings flowing like a swift river, my thoughts dancing like sunlight on the page. But I couldn't write on it because I don't write that way. I can stare at the typewriter for hours, trying to dredge up a solitary truth from the swamps of me, just trying to see into those dark and murky depths. Writing, rewriting, I'm satisfied after a morning's work with one paragraph that doesn't lie; I don't need electronics for that.

I'm writing this on another typewriter, an aging, neglected portable we had at the office. Though it doesn't hum or blink at me, it's not my Underwood, and, with the pounding I'm giving it, it probably won't last.

Meanwhile, the Underwood sits where it always has, on the old maple typing table beside my desk. I know I need to haul it to the dumpster, toss it in. I don't know what I'm waiting for. Maybe for the soul to pass, before letting the body rest in peace. Maybe because it's hard to say goodbye to the rows of silent keys.

ENEMIES OF FREEDOM

I T'S ODD WHAT I REMEMBER: the weather, sunny and brisk; the red-tiled roofs awash with light, shining as if they'd been scrubbed the night before. I remember the excitement, dark like some forbidden sexual thrill, of breaking the rules, being here on the quad instead of in class. Two thirds of us boycotted our classes that day because the college administration had banned a Communist from speaking on campus. We marched. We gave speeches about the hypocrisy and the infuriating paternalism of banning a speaker at a liberal arts college dedicated to the habits of freedom.

I remember the rumors that grew more ominous as the day went on, like the shadows lengthening across the quad: FBI agents were among us; they were taking down names; they were hiding behind trees, taking pictures. This would go on our record. Not just our college record, as if that weren't worry enough, but *the* record, kept somewhere in Washington, of the subversives and the Commies, where they put down your name like a brand on cattle, and you like an old cow with no power to complain.

I didn't like that at all. I'd never been in trouble with the police or my teachers or anyone. The closest I'd come to an act of seeming disobedience was in the third grade, when I got separated from my class during a fire drill. I panicked. I started running down the hall, praying I would find them. A fire drill, after all, was a ritual so awesome, so shrouded in silence and high gloom, that we might as well have been in a temple or a church. Who knew what wrath I was calling down on my little self?

Maybe, I thought, they'd taken the stairs. I raced down those iron stairs, two at a time, my heart racing, too — and as I wheeled around the second-floor landing, I ran into them, into my amused classmates and my humorless teacher, coming up the same stairs.

I got off with only a reprimand, but it was a profoundly unsettling moment, as if I'd fallen from grace. I'd been taught all my life to be good, to follow the rules — left like markers to guide me through the thickets, to lead me away from the wrong friends and the wrong feelings and the wrong foods. My life was circumscribed by laws as old as Moses and as new as my parents' latest whim, a tangle of rules and regulations I'd need a lawyer to sort out, if they weren't already written on my brain. I rarely broke the rules. If I did, I was scolded, in a way that usually made me feel I'd been spanked. "This is no democracy," my father would remind me. Of course, he meant our family, not the whole country. But when we're children, our family is our country and our world, and the rules my parents laid down stretched as far as I could see.

Not surprisingly, by the time I got to college, I was appallingly conscientious and studious and, like most of my classmates, generally willing to do what I was told; rebellion wasn't yet the fashion. In 1961, we were still rubbing from our eyes the long sleep of the Eisenhower years, and the wretched nightmare of McCarthyism. People were being tested for loyalty, not drugs, though perhaps it's all the same.

As students, we endured tests that were more mundane, tests for literature and history and philosophy — those courses meant to introduce us to the depth and breadth of western culture and to the life of the mind, to broaden us and burden us with more ideas than we knew what to do with. Were we meant to take them seriously? Did our teachers take them seriously? When we asked our teachers and our deans and the president of the college to take seriously a great idea like freedom, we found out.

In banning a Communist from speaking, in refusing to give a forum to an enemy of freedom, the college made itself an enemy of freedom. Ironically, had the talk been permitted, not many students would have gone. Except for a small group of campus leftists, more committed to late-night bull sessions than to overthrowing the government, very few of us cared about Marxist politics. But by giving in to pressure from right-wing groups, the college set the stage for a controversy that would drag on for months.

It set the stage, too, for a change in me. Like the breeze that blew through the campus that day, whipping up the leaves and our hair, the student strike stirred me. Certainly, in deciding to march despite my fears, I woke up a little: I saw more clearly that my teachers weren't my parents and my parents weren't God and that I could risk a little disapproval without having my world fall apart. And if I was wrong — if my world did fall apart? Well, I didn't know about that. But I did know that unless I made a stand for something important to me, I'd fall into a deeper and more baneful sleep, from which I might never wake up.

I began to consider more keenly the perils of limiting dissent in a democracy, of skimping on freedom as if there were only so much to go around. The real patriots, it seemed to me, weren't those who insisted that truth, *their* truth, be defended at any cost — or who suggested, with a wink at history, that our rights would best be protected by stripping us of a few. Democracy asks for a sturdier faith, asks us to trust that in the free discussion of ideas, truth will more often than not win out. What a dangerous notion, to those who prize above all else security and a predictable tomorrow. It's as risky as love. Yet, miraculously, among people of different backgrounds and temperaments, different races and religions — people as different as you and I — the spirit of truth somehow prevails. Not *my* truth or *your* truth, but something shared, an understanding between equals, at once mystical and practical, that allows us to live together. Like a friendship or a marriage, democracy depends on communication and trust. Yes, we know the risks. If we're free to love, we're free to hate — free to be Communists and Nazis and Democrats and Republicans and every kind of fool. John Adams advised, "There's a danger from all men. The only maxim of a free government ought to be to trust no man living with the power to endanger the public liberty."

I value the lessons I learned that year about freedom and its enemies. As a writer and an editor — for my college paper, later for a daily newspaper, and now for *The Sun* — I don't take freedom for granted. To be able to write and speak freely, without fear of censorship or reprisal, is, for me, a gift greater than any fame or fortune the writing may bring. To let the mind roam, to move to my own rhythms instead of those of some committee, to be led to unexpected conclusions by the very act of putting the inexpressible into words — this is precious *beyond* words.

I'm fascinated by the power of words to move us to action and laughter and tears. I'm fascinated by what gives words their meaning and their glory, what lights them from within. After all, the words themselves, the letters on the page, don't contain any meaning, but are merely symbols; only if we agree on the symbols, if we share certain beliefs about what is and isn't real, do the words make sense. Language reflects back to us our deepest assumptions about the world and ourselves.

So, too, are our political institutions mirrors, reflecting back to us our shared beliefs. For two hundred years, we've cherished a belief in freedom, notwithstanding the abuses of demagogues and charlatans, propagandists and pornographers. No doubt about it: people free to express themselves generously are free to make mistakes, free to become ensnared and to ensnare others in the most humiliating illusions, and free also to learn and change and grow. Just as our inner journey is a passage out of darkness — a halting and perilous adventure, full of folly, on our way to truth — so, too, as a people do we stumble and fall.

Edwin Meese, the attorney general, attacks the Constitution as if it were a document of questionable taste. He calls for startling restrictions on freedom of expression, challenges key rights of the accused, pushes for a lifetime censorship of government workers as a way of stifling dissent. The president himself acts as if an informed citizenry were dangerous, as if democracy itself were a threat.

When the president is an enemy of freedom, when the "friends" of freedom are broadcasting and publishing monopolies — for whom the First Amendment is a license to see how much profit they can make — it's tempting to feel despair. Surely, as individuals and as a people, we've become comfortable, sleepy. I was given a pointed reminder recently of just how drowsy and complacent one can get.

I received a letter from the American Civil Liberties Union, asking for my signature as *The Sun*'s editor on a petition calling for the removal from office of Attorney General Meese. Since Reagan is Meese's boss, it was a symbolic effort, but that didn't matter; the idea was to take a stand.

I was about to sign, but I hesitated. I didn't want to get on anyone's list. I didn't want to pay the price for a reckless moment, for a gesture so obviously futile I wondered if my signature was even worth a stamp. Besides, I had a magazine to worry about, which, because it's nonprofit and tax-exempt, isn't allowed to try to influence any legislation. Might my signing such a petition be considered lobbying and thus illegal? I didn't think so, but I wasn't sure. What if the attorney general himself decided subtle legal questions such as this?

I set the letter aside, promising myself I'd think about it. When I picked it up again a few days later, the memory of the student strike came back to me, shining a warning across the years.

It's easy to get depressed by the compromises others make, to grow melancholy because the language has been stripped of its majesty by the same kind of mentality that strip-mines the land. It's not so easy to see my own compromises, how I give away freedom for comfort and approval and to cultivate an image of myself as sensitive and wise; yes, here on the page so handsome a man. How tempting not to risk this image with some really embarrassing disclosure, or to risk my magazine's tax-exempt status with some controversial stand. My fear tells me to set aside the ACLU letter. My fear threatens my freedom as much as do Reagan and Meese.

I signed the petition and sent it off. Then I realized that despite all my memories about the strike, I couldn't remember how it turned out. Did the administration eventually give in? You'd think I'd remember something that important, but I don't. I remember the hesitation, the daring.

BY THE BEAUTIFUL SEA

SOON WE'LL BE BY THE SEA AGAIN.

Like pilgrims we come each year, my wife and her son and my daughters and I. It's a family tradition for our sometimes-family. Each summer, for a week, we come here to have fun, before saying goodbye to the waves and the summer and each other: Jaime going back to his father in New Jersey; Mara and Sara going back to their mother in the mountains; Norma and I going back to an unencumbered life which full-time parents sometimes envy, but not as much as we envy theirs.

What is there to envy, though? We think we understand someone's life but we never understand; our joys and griefs can't be compared. Only from a distance, and through the haze of ignorance, do we judge and praise and condemn.

See us walking along the beach, on a hazy morning, a family on vacation, Dad and Mom and the kids.

My arm is around Norma's waist; the curves of our bodies fit. The children are lithe and healthy-looking. They search for shells; they watch a gull skimming the waves; they're happy here.

We walk, I talk about something I've just read or am worried about. Norma half-listens, wondering why I tax my mind so, wishing I were more fully here with the sky and the sea. She bends to pick up a shell — dark, wet, nearly perfect — and hands it to me.

The children want to show me their shells, too. I look at each one, marveling at their strange beauty, with the waves breaking and roaring nearby and the water hissing around our feet. I think, for a moment, how important Norma and I and the children are to each other, yet, in this vast landscape, how insignificant; how loved we are and how lonely; family and speck. There's an old Hasidic saying that a man must have two pockets to reach into: in his right pocket, he must keep the words "For my sake was the world created"; in his left, "I am dust and ash."

There's another paradox for me in being here, spiraling like a conch shell from an event nearly forty years in my past. Like the sea, ever-changing and never-changing, I come back each year different but the same. The fear is the same, so old it seems a part of me, like my hands or my face. The paradox is that I love and hate the sea — that I'm drawn to it with a passion, but won't go in above my knees.

I never learned to swim. I nearly drowned as a child, or so it seemed to me. What really happened — since my father is dead now — will always be a mystery.

The family was on vacation in the country, at a lake surrounded by trees. In the middle was an old-fashioned, wooden, weather-beaten raft. One day, my father hoisted me on his back and swam out to it with me.

He was a fat man but a strong swimmer; I loved the way he moved, the feel of him beneath me, the long, powerful strokes. At the age of four or five, I loved everything about him.

The raft, when we got there, was already crowded. He treaded water, his arm around me, while he and the other swimmers talked and joked.

Suddenly, he let go. It was unbelievable, like a dark door appearing out of nowhere, opening and then shutting behind me, leaving me in a room of water without ceiling, walls, or floor. I started sinking. My thrashing brought me up like a buoy. I gasped for air. I started sinking again. I thrashed some more.

I don't know how long this went on, but I remember vividly the helplessness, the disbelief. What had happened? How in the world could he have let go?

Hands reached out for me; to this day I don't know whose. Maybe they were my father's, lifting me out of the water, but they felt like a stranger's hands, comforting me, not sure where I belonged. By this time, I was crying hysterically. I heard my father's voice, and looked up, and he was holding me. Between sobs, I pleaded with him to take me back to shore.

I was still crying when we got there. My mother asked what was wrong. "It was nothing," he said. Someone had splashed me and I'd "panicked." I looked at him, dumbfounded. "But Dad! You let go!" He shook his head. He said I was making a big deal out of nothing, and told me to stop crying. Something sank in me then, swifter than my own body in the water.

I still don't understand what happened that day, either in the water or between us as father and son.

His story was implausible, less convincing than a fairy tale. But it was frightening to admit, even to myself, that he might be telling a lie. Being unable to trust him was as terrifying, in its way, as drowning. As children, we need to believe our parents. It's impossible for us to understand they're still struggling with childhood fears of their own.

The dilemma comes when we have to choose between them and ourselves — between their truth and our reality, their idea of love and our injured hearts. Something we know, some feeling we have, *who we are*, isn't acceptable to them. The pain of that is enormous; for a small child, it's too great to live with. So it's buried under a false self that fits in with their beliefs. For me, being afraid all these years of the water was safer than being afraid of my father.

How many fears are like this. How many wounds we receive from parents themselves too wounded to give us what we need. The wounds scab over, but life picks at the scabs. For me, it happens every year at the sea.

EASY ANSWER

To TEST MY NEW answerng machine, I call myself at the office as soon as I get home. The recorded announcement says I'm not there. I reply, "Of course you're not." Norma laughs from the next room. For several weeks, with growing amusement and some dismay, she's been listening to me evaluate all the answering machines and their features: automatic redialing, remote playback, and — Norma, get this — a speakerphone that lets you carry on a conversation from anywhere in the room.

When I get to the office the next morning, I check to see if the machine really works. The volume control, turned up too high, makes my voice boom like one of those embarrassingly loud announcements that used to come over the school PA system, making everyone snicker at the principal's ineptitude with the mike. I lower the volume, satisfied I've made the right choice — the sleek buttons, the reassuring sophistication of flashing lights and digital readouts, evoking that heady sense of proud ownership.

I'm not sure what all the buttons are for, not having had time to read the thirty-page instruction booklet. Indeed, I can't say what's more amazing to me: the gadgets or my fascination with them. It's not like me to get this excited over a machine. I know that for some people there's poetry in mechanics or electronics, a delight in discovering what makes things work. While I admire that quality, and wish I were more handy, for me there's more poetry in poetry. Besides, I'm suspicious of machines. So many of them seem to bruise the spirit, deceiving us with lies about our illusory power. Other machines seem benign until we become dependent on them. We did this with cars. Now we're doing it with computers, having convinced ourselves that our survival depends on how quickly we can move data from terminal to terminal and from one confused soul to the next.

Years ago, I imagined my preference for a simpler life — heating with wood, washing the dishes by hand, growing a few vegetables without sprays or chemical fertilizer — made my life more authentic, set me apart from a culture enamored of progress.

It was a conceit that had less to do with the advantages or disadvantages of wood heat or organic gardening than with the need to be a little different, a little better. How tempting it was to romanticize my wholesome values, my fashionably old-fashioned style — but this was to confuse the look of a life with looking deeply into life. How ironic that I saw such posturing as evidence my life was more authentic — but I always find a story more convincing when the hero is me. Less heroic, though perhaps more authentic, were the deeply troubled and destructive aspects of my own nature.

I'm reminded of the Luddites, who roamed England in the nineteenth century, smashing textile machines, hoping they could stave off the Industrial Revolution and preserve authentic village life . . . and of IBM, in the 1980s, dreaming of a global village linked by computers. Seemingly worlds apart, these visions share an uncompromising faith in the power of technology, making it something to worship or fear. Both, in their wish to save the world, ignore the human heart, which tells us we need first to save ourselves. The tools for this are available to everyone, but it's pick-and-shovel work under a scorching sun, and we find as many opportunities as possible to distract ourselves, and call it progress.

It's not surprising. We imagine our eyes are windows, through which we see reality, but our eyes are more like mirrors, reflecting back our own beliefs. Perhaps we acknowledge this on some level — seeing how childhood shapes and haunts grown-up friendships and loves — but can't see how it's true of everything: politics, economics, the environment, everything we call real and believe to be more real than our inner realm, the peaks and valleys of emotions, the ancient landscape of ideas.

Thus, my wife, studying to be a doctor, ponders the appropriate use of machines to keep the dying alive a little longer, sometimes against their own will. Medical technology seems to have redrawn the boundary between life and death; doctors, perplexed medically and ethically, feel like pawns in technology's controlling hand.

To take another, more universal example, we all feel like pawns who may be sacrificed at any time: nuclear weapons, supposed to protect us, have become meaningless as a means of defense; using them seals our fate. Thus, technology apparently redraws boundaries again.

Such dilemmas, seemingly the consequence of technology, may be seen instead as artful symbols created by the mind, terrifying new ways to confront age-old fears. Evidently, the stakes get higher the faster we run from ourselves, avoiding the really important questions — who we are, why we're here. After all, physicians whose only goal is keeping us alive are merely convinced (like the rest of us) that we're these bodies (like a driver insisting he's his car). And when we recoil from nuclear weapons, and blame Reagan or the Russians for the fix we're in, we might consider the immeasurable destructive power in each of us, and whether the bomb is any more or less evil than ourselves. When have we not made war, or prayed for wars to end? A computer error may start the next war, but what error started us on this war within, each part of our nature denying the rest, until our soul was divided like so many countries, armed and dangerous, ready to kill?

How much easier to blame technology than to stand before the mirror, not averting our gaze, or to sit quietly, steadfastly refusing to turn from what's inside us: the conditioning and anxiety and fear. Talk about pollution! Talk about a world where we use nuclear power to boil water for electricity (which, as Amory Lovins said, is like using a chainsaw to cut butter) and then look at the tremendous mental energy each of us expends on petty grievances, little worries, protecting who we think we are — with the past for a sword and the future for a shield.

We're frightened of life, which our technology will never explain or control. In the aftermath of the Challenger disaster, with everyone trying to figure out what went wrong, we all know what really went wrong, what always goes wrong: the unexpected happens; someone suffers; someone dies. Then there's grief, also uncontrollable, and thank God for that. After the crash, if only for a moment, explanations weren't needed, faces were unmasked. Like a family that needs a funeral to bring it together, we all paused briefly. It was not only Christa McAuliffe and her six companions we eulogized, but also ourselves, and our parents and children and friends. For a moment, we were reminded of how brief our lives are, and how much we don't understand. Then we shrugged and slipped behind our masks, ignoring again the countless other tragedies around us, the questions technology can't answer.

Last winter, when I started brooding about how compulsively I eat, I became depressed. I started eating more compulsively, which led to feeling guilty, which led to overeating again. How discouraging. I'm a man gifted with words, who communicates ideas and feelings, but this was like talking to myself in a language I couldn't understand.

My interest in getting a new answering machine started then. Maybe being depressed had nothing to do with it. Still, I wonder: during a difficult time, when I felt inarticulate and incomplete, when *I couldn't get through to myself,* I bought an answering machine that dials and redials, lights up and beeps, and lets me leave "personal memos."

Now that I have it, I'm learning to use it. That's the nature of technology, which is why the bomb seems like such a threat. The real threat, I think, is our reluctance to listen. The heart asks all the right questions, and we play deaf.

THE SHADOW'S SPEED

I WAS TALKING WITH A FRIEND the other day about marriage, and how hard it is to make a marriage last, how it can seem as futile as trying to make the morning last, or trying to make that first kiss — the one that seemed to go on forever — go on forever.

My friend had just gotten married, so the subject was on her mind. It's never far from my mind — I've been married three times — but during the past year, five couples I know have split up. The death of a marriage is like the death of a person: who my friends were together is gone. Memories are left, but they'll soon be gone, too. How shadowy we become, to those we loved and who loved us. Time passes; the distance gathers around us; unforgettable days and nights are forgotten, and go where they go, and are gone.

Married only a few weeks, my friend was naturally hopeful her own marriage would last. But her day had started badly, with an argument that rose from the breakfast table like a rocket out of control. She and her husband had been planning to move to another city, thousands of miles away; it was his idea, to which she had reluctantly agreed. Now she wasn't so sure. They had discussed it many times. It was no longer a difference of opinion but an issue, threatening to become an impasse. They were smart enough to know no one really wins an argument like this, but they weren't smart enough not to argue. Who is? We forget what missiles our words are, how much damage we can cause with one thoughtless comment between the coffee and the toast.

The real issue, my friend said, wasn't whether or not they'd move. It was that her husband's mind was already made up. She felt powerless, which frightened her, but when she tried to talk to him about how she felt, it frightened him. He was threatened, she said, by her seeming indecision; he felt he couldn't trust her. Still, she wasn't discouraged.

That's good, I thought. In the face of such complex feelings, it would be tempting to get discouraged. After all, people throw away computerized watches and radios and tape recorders when they break down because they're too complicated to fix; it's cheaper to buy a new one. So, too, are relationships discarded, with the compelling argument that human nature is too complex. We're certainly more complex than any computer, programmed as we are with contradictory needs and longings, childhood memories that shape our adult lives but are too painful to recall, knowledge and ignorance forever braided. Our understanding of human nature, and of our conditioned ways of thinking and feeling, is so partial that most of us can't live peacefully with ourselves, let alone with someone else. We swing from wild optimism to silent despair about the world, about relationships. We're complex beyond imagining: thoughts leap from mind to mind, and who can say why? Love leaps from heart to heart. Something else leaps, too. As Howard Nemerov writes, "Nothing in the universe can travel at the speed of light, they say, forgetful of the shadow's speed."

My friend explained that she and her husband were "different personality types" with different fears — hers being "loss of love" and his "annihilation." As long as they kept this in mind, they could learn to understand and accept each other.

I said these didn't sound like different fears so much as different ways of describing the same fear. We all flinch from death and loss; from the things we sweated out as children; from the old griefs that climb the heart like grasses, swept by changing moods and life's vagrant winds. Fear has a thousand names when it's ourselves we fear. Convinced of our separateness, we separate ourselves yet further; we create categories, differences, types.

She said I didn't understand. She described to me the theory of the Russian mystic Gurdjieff, who elaborated nine different personality types. Each type represented a unique constellation of beliefs, a distinct way of thinking and feeling and moving. Gurdjieff's insights, she said, had broadened her understanding of how people affect each other. What could I say? To accept each other's differences, in a world of enmity and strife, is important. If

Gurdjieff or astrology or the *I Ching* or the Tarot help us to do that, we're better off. We live in an age in which the proliferation of traditionally secret teachings is unprecedented. There are, too, the techniques taught by our modern-day gurus, the psychotherapists. Never has so much information — some of it admittedly silly but much of it stunningly sophisticated and wise — been available to ordinary people. And never has the divorce rate been so high.

I don't mean to sound cynical, or to ridicule the good sense of my friend. Cynicism is certainly out of place; it's nothing but the cry of the die-hard romantic who clings to his illusions and berates others for not living up to them. After all, who scorns hope and innocence and tender affection more than the lost soul whose need to be cared for is so great? Who scoffs at marriage more bitterly than the man or woman who a few years ago swore an undying love?

No, I mean only to suggest that a theory is a theory and living is something else. My friends who split up this year had their theories, too. They struggled to understand life, too. When the facts didn't fit the theories, they revised the theories. They searched for the missing clue, for the theory that would explain why none of the theories worked. Eventually, they had to ignore the facts or abandon the theories — a painful choice, since lies break the heart, and so does the truth.

I have my theories, revised countless times since I first walked down the aisle, nearly twenty years ago, in top hat and tails. How preposterous I must have looked. But it was, after all, the style: like sentimentalizing love and making a fantasy of my wife; like ignoring the astonishing power over our lives of our parents' unlived lives, the ineluctable pull of the past; like our shameless obedience to traditional roles. My wife worked and did the housework, while I worked and thought about important things. I never washed a dish.

Am I the same man who tonight, even as I clean up after dinner, is thinking about what to make my wife for lunch? I've found the splendor in the ordinary. What a lucky man! My soul isn't out there in the sky, or in the vast sweep of my thoughts, but here, fresh and close by — in the light the small lamp throws on the shadows of the kitchen and on the old, scarred cutting board and on the slices of bread.

It's a perfect moment, dark and suspended like the pause between breaths. Norma is across the room. I look at her. How real and mysterious she is, in her delights and her sorrows. But moments come and go, like theories, like Norma and I in our lives too busy by half. We're in and out the door, she to the hospital by six, I to the office before that. Sometimes days go by without any real intimacy, without either of us bringing an unfamiliar mood to the table, a question to our certainty, a sweet new cunning to the bed. We strive for a life together — for the ordered virtues, for our share of bliss — but we have to take risks with each other, risk the marriage itself, for a life together to make sense.

At least, that's the theory. Another has to do with telling the truth, always; and another with the redemptive power of forgiveness; and another with the need to accept. Unfortunately, when the comforting illusion of a comforting love is torn away, the theories are forgotten. When I'm tired or bruised or angry, my refuge isn't truth and forgiveness. If the world doesn't feed me, if things go wrong, if I've spent my day in the shallows of myself, the pull of the lie is strong. My mind, not my heart, speaks for me then, like a shyster lawyer full of empty words. I wink at the jury. I smile at the judge. I forget that the verdict came in on this pretending long ago.

If I start a conversation with Norma by disguising what I feel, I usually end up scolding her for holding back what she feels. This is like Reagan frothing over Qaddafi's duplicity. Fortunately, I don't do this often; when I do, my wife reminds me we're pledged to something higher than diplomacy. But what happens when both of us are unsure what we feel, when the heart is a distant land and we're nearsighted with the desire to please? What good are theories when you can't tell the loneliness from the boredom and the boredom from the lust?

I was sick the other night, too weary to build a fire. Norma was at the hospital ministering to other sick people — an irony that, in my fevered state, held undue fascination for me. My throat burned each time I swallowed; I couldn't concentrate on my book and there was nothing on TV. Heavy and sad, I drifted in and out of sleep, wanting something sleep couldn't give me.

I wanted to feel cared for, but I didn't know what to do for myself. It's an old story. I see illness as a sign of weakness. Men in particular, I think, suffer from this slander; it makes sickness a kind of failure and "caring for yourself" an empty ritual, devoid of generosity. More generally, I'm not much of a friend when the friend in need is me. When I'm sick or tired or discouraged, I look inside myself for comfort, and a scornful ghost looks back at me. It's a look I can't bear, and like a frightened child I run from it, to a woman, to rescue me. Wife, mother, savior, her life becomes the screen on which I project my need. I want to see nothing but her great love for me.

When Norma finally got home, I was sullen and unfriendly, spurning the affection she offered me. Nothing she said or did was quite enough. Just as intractable as my weepy eyes and stuffy nose was my dour mood. In bed, we kept to our separate sides. Oh, the dark ruin of a bed when you go to sleep angry.

BREATHING SPACE

JOHN AND I work in the old yellow house on West Rosemary Street, where *The Sun* and Lunar Graphics are located. We're an odd couple, thrown together by circumstance. He's intelligent, articulate when he wants to be, but shy, and tends not to talk much about himself. I'm more expressive and outgoing, more emotional — to a fault, John suggests.

For the most part, we get along. After all, we share some overriding concerns. He, too, left New York in search of a life, not merely a living. Sometimes, while waiting for the morning coffee to brew, we talk if we're not too busy. Sometimes days go by without much being said. We're like neighbors who meet rarely over the back-yard fence, but keep an eye on each other nonetheless.

What was it John saw when he looked my way a few weeks ago? Just how much do people speak to each other without speaking? What do our bodies say, brushing past each other in the hall?

Maybe he didn't see anything, but was prompted by some odd inner summons to leave that article on my desk. John rarely gives me things to read, but friends are often unwitting messengers, their unsuspecting words or gestures telling us what we need to hear.

The article was by a local businessman who turns away customers to have more time for his family and for himself, who disdains conventional notions of work and success. He wrote of staying small "not because I couldn't get the business," but because too much growth "would have changed me in ways I didn't want to change."

Did I need a reminder that life is more than our accomplishments; that all our accomplishments are here, then gone, like a breath that fogs the glass? Buildings crumble, lovers part, everything born dies. How odd, this striving to be successful, here between the breaths.

How odd, and how human. I, too, disdain worldly success. But my own ambitions — to be a better writer, a better editor — create the same pitch of self-absorption, drive me to the same brink of exhaustion as the investment banker who falls asleep with a calculator in his hand.

On the same morning John put the article on my desk, I'd gotten up hours before dawn to finish my latest essay. Since my deadline was fast approaching, I decided to stay at home and devote the whole day to writing, free of phone calls and interruptions, little counting on how big an interruption I myself would become.

For several weeks, I'd been troubled by a tightness in my chest — a subtle pressure, like someone's hand resting there — and I'd had difficulty taking a full, deep breath. The sensation would come and go, for reasons that continued to elude me. I rarely felt it when I ran; sometimes, though, I'd wake up and my first breath would be labored; other times, I wouldn't feel it until late in the day.

It wasn't the first time I'd had this problem. Years ago, after splitting up with a girlfriend, I developed identical symptoms. Thinking I was having a heart attack, I rushed to the clinic, to be assured my heart, though wounded, was quite healthy, and that I'd live to hurt again. What was wrong with me, then? Nothing physical, the doctor said; it was anxiety. It was my own troubled psyche pressing down on me, giving me no room to breathe. Threatened by my feelings, I had imagined my very life was in danger. In a way it was: the life I'd known with this woman was over. Yet how hard it was to accept. Instead of mourning our losses, we deny them. We betray our feelings, then — surprise — our bodies betray us.

Over the years, like a troublesome visitor who shows up at my front door without any warning, the symptoms return, for days or weeks. Breathing becomes a puzzle, a science I haven't mastered. I don't cough or wheeze; I just can't seem to get enough air. The sensation is oppressive; so, too, is the burden of figuring out why my body does this to me. Sometimes, the answer is evident; sometimes it's a mystery I can't penetrate — the emotions too painful, the denial too great.

On the day I stayed at home — a sultry, humid Friday in early

June — I sat looming all morning over my little empire of scribbled notes and paper and pencils and coffee, while my impending deadline loomed over me. I've lived with deadlines most of my life, celebrating each day with one eye on the hour hand. Too busy to curl up at night with a good book instead of a stack of manuscripts, too busy to get a full night's sleep, too busy to take a day off to wander in the woods — this isn't what I had in mind when I started *The Sun*. I meet my deadlines. But too often, in the service of some higher purpose, I ignore my body's rhythms — its subtle (and not-so-subtle) deadlines, its whispered plea to pause, to rest, to reflect.

As I labored over my essay that morning, my breathing grew more and more burdened. Breathing should be effortless. Instead, it was a weight, a worry, each breath like a rusty swing banging against something unyielding, its arc never completed, my lungs never full.

I got up from the desk and lay on the bed. It's the lack of sleep, the coffee, the anxiety, I reasoned — half hoping the diagnosis itself would dispel the symptoms, but they only got worse. I tried harder and harder to take a deep breath, expanding my chest, inhaling forcefully, trying to will the air inside. No longer able to ignore my distress, feeling helpless and frightened, I began to panic. What for weeks had been worrisome, a gathering storm on the horizon, was now raging all around me. Thoughts flew like branches snapped by the wind: God was punishing me; I was going to die; maybe I wouldn't die but would go on suffering, forever uncertain why.

Try to relax, my wife implored. She said I was hyperventilating, which was making me lightheaded and anxious. God doesn't punish us, she said, but the words made no sense to me. You're not going to die, she said, but the fear drowned her out, laying waste to reason, a monstrous machine with its own momentum, mowing me down.

And down I went, terrified and cringing, into some wild part of me, the lip of madness, a roiling darkness where words didn't matter, where all that mattered was one thing: not to die.

Norma stared at me as I leapt from the bed. I knew where I was going; I knew it without thinking, the way a cry rises from the chest. I knew, as I clambered down the stairs and burst out the door, that I needed to be outside — out of the house, out of my mind, out of the life of the mind that had become so airless. What I longed for in that moment, with a wild desperation, was *life*, not my symbols for it. I wanted the dark earth that grew things, the sheltering trees and their shadows, the grass, the leaves, the thick summer air. I ran to the garden — Norma's garden, where, too busy for gardening, I rarely ventured. I sank down on my hands and knees, and buried my hands in the soil. It wasn't "nature" I wanted, not some abstraction, but the sustenance, the strength and comfort of the living earth itself. And there, in the dirt, on my knees, sobbing, I was able to breathe again.

SHE CALLED THE OTHER DAY. She was reading something that reminded her of me, she said. How long had it been since we'd talked? Two years? Three years?

Such a simple and mysterious thing, to call someone — to pick up a phone, dial a number, and summon from across the miles and years a voice, a presence, the familiarity of a time long gone. How amazing to be sitting at your desk, absorbed in your thoughts, and the next moment to be communicating with someone far away, your minds arching across space and time, unaccountably joining what a moment before was separate. Is distance real? When we touch each other, in a moment of understanding, isn't the physical universe of crippling distances and lost memories for a moment repealed? We take it for granted — as we do most things — seeing a phone as "just" a phone, a conversation as a string of words, but to call someone is an act of pure magic, an act as intimate, as tender and reckless, as reaching across the table to give a perfect stranger a kiss.

Our conversation took me back to the time we met, nearly thirteen years ago, on a cold day, on a highway.

Hitchhiking's golden age was already in eclipse by then, but its allure was still great. The road was the best kind of guru, winding through you wordlessly, teaching through experience. The lessons were different for each of us: as different as our lives, our stories, the innocence or the cynicism in our eyes; as different as the lines around our eyes, telltale road maps of where we'd been.

Along the interstate or beside a truck stop or out beyond the run-down edge of town, you stood with your thumb out, or holding a piece of cardboard ripped from an old box, on which you'd scrawled in big, black letters where you wanted to go: Boulder or L.A. or, simply, Canada or West Coast. But no matter how careful with the magic marker you were, the ink would spread over the corrugated ridges like a stream overflowing its banks. It would run in tiny rivulets and make your sign a mess. Hitchhiking was messy, messy and human, like great cities, and great loves, and the great days of your life. You'd fold and refold your map, certain of what lay ahead, and somehow end up on a serpentine back road that went nowhere. And, after an hour or two or three in the biting cold or the merciless sun, waiting for the next ride you knew would never come — convinced you'd have to walk to the next town or sleep that night by the side of the road — you were ready to admit how foolish this was, ready to give up, ready to go home.

And it was then, at the very moment you'd had it with this aching world, with its blindness and its deafness and its utter disregard for your aching heart (and your aching feet) that you heard a car. Impossible! And it was slowing, as if the planet itself were slowing in its mindless turning. And it was stopping, to a hallelujah of crunching gravel. Life was stopping. Love was skidding to a halt in front of you, and winking at you. Only kidding, love said. Hadn't forgotten you, love said. Just wanted to see if you'd forgotten. Hop in.

I cherish that time in my life for the adventures, the friendships, the unexpected mercies — but mostly, because I learned to trust the road. Trusting the road meant not forgetting what waits just out of sight. Possibility and compassion aren't on the map. Our senses may deny them. Indeed, along the desolate highway, or deep in the city, or anywhere we're faced with ugliness and despair, love can seem like an illusion, beguiling and cruel. Perhaps, we think, we knew it as a child, but it's lost now; perhaps the memory of it haunts us; perhaps we see glimpses of it but don't trust it, and so are afraid to trust anything or anyone. Trust the road? Don't be silly. It's unpredictable, remorseless. It winds on endlessly, like the future. You can't see around the next bend.

For me, hitchhiking was as much an inner as an outer journey, teaching me that every step we take is metaphoric of some movement within. I was leaving behind a way of thinking that insisted on certain boundaries — boundaries I'd always contemplated nervously, like sailors before Columbus gazing fearfully at that distant rim. The world was flat; they had proof of it.

I was nearly thirty years old then, with two college degrees, and books from floor to ceiling, but I was just beginning to understand one of life's most important lessons: that what we call the world is made up of sights and sounds and shadows from our private world, from our past, from the taboos on feeling and thinking we learned before we could even talk; that whatever we seek or fear out there is, in fact, something within; that our beliefs shape our reality as surely as a potter's hands shape clay.

Trusting the road was a potent symbol of my journey within a journey. To shoulder my pack and walk out to the highway with no idea of how long it would take to get where I was going — or whether I would get there at all — forced me, as someone who had always angled for the sure thing, to take another look at my trusted (but untrusting) frame of reference. Nothing in it could account for being driven several hundred miles by someone who never stops for hitchhikers; for being put up at night by perfect strangers without having asked; for being fed. Once, someone drove more than a hundred miles out of his way to carry me right to my destination. As an Italian proverb would have it, "For a web begun, God sends thread."

There was, too, the generosity of open and sympathetic minds, of companionship that was sudden and improbable. How often I'd be alone beside the road, car after car passing me by, alone with my solitary thoughts and a big, cloudless sky. And a car would stop. I'd get inside. I'd smile at the person behind the wheel. He or she would smile back. And I knew, though it made no sense, I was with an old friend.

I'd heard it said, when I started on my journey, that *the road takes care*. This struck me as naive, another sixties myth. But before long, I was invoking it myself. Myth it might be, but I preferred it to a myth of despair. If I was wrong, I figured the news would catch up with me, but after all these years, and all these miles, it hasn't yet.

I rarely hitchhike these days, and I don't miss the highway — perhaps because I keep finding new places and new companions within. The wandering turns to wondering. I travel other roads: my magazine, my marriage, raising my children. They wind through different parts of me, and teach in different ways. But the rules of the road stay the same.

As to the phone call that brought back these memories, there's little to say. We didn't talk much, even in the old days. She was a teacher for me, though, of silence, of letting nature speak to you and for you — languages I still don't understand.

As to how we met, I'm reminded of an image from a Chinese fairy tale: lovers are attached to each other from birth by invisible strings. One night, in moonlight, the strings become visible, red lines on their wrists. The strings shorten until the two lovers meet on a bridge.

Which is to say, I have no idea what brought us together, what brings any two people together, to love each other for a while and go their separate ways. Invisible strings are one explanation.

Here's another: it was a cold day, on a highway. She stopped to give me a ride.

COMPANY

IT'S THE HEART OF OUR KITCHEN — an ordinary table, made of sturdy pine boards, solidly joined, built to last. Though it's scarred and scratched, Norma says she likes it that way. She wants to read our history on it, the way you read the lines on someone's face.

The table is the mirror of our domestic order, and disorder: the meals we eat with our mismatched silver; the children doing homework; Norma kneading and pounding dough into bread; the late-night talks about the uncertain future; the games of backgammon and chess. It's where we gather with friends, as we did recently. We were finishing dinner, the kitchen rich with the mingled aromas of garlic, oil, the wood fire in the next room, the children's freshly washed hair, all the smells that belonged to the house as we belonged to each other — family and friends talking and laughing, a circle of human warmth in the darkness of a winter night, when the talk, unexpectedly, turned into a discussion; and then, with unmistakable emphasis, into an argument; and then, dismayingly, into an argument about arguing itself.

Does it matter how it started? How do you trace an argument, which never follows a straight line? Someone says something that lays back the scab of an old wound; hurt turns into anger; emotions loop around each other, past and present incestuously entwined.

We had been talking about something in the news, about distant lives made suddenly important, symbolic. A woman had been told her baby wasn't going to live. Doctors said it was anencephalic — most of its brain was missing — and there was nothing they could do; such babies die within hours after birth, as one organ after another fails. But the mother had insisted that the baby be kept alive on a respirator — even though it had no chance of surviving — until another infant needed one of its organs, and a successful transplant could be made. God had told her to do this, she said. It would mean her baby wouldn't die in vain.

Would the baby suffer as a result? No one around the table knew. Opinion was divided over whether any suffering was justified, however slight. Opinion was further divided over the thorny issue of organ transplants, and the social and moral dilemmas modern medicine inspires. Medical technology has created new heavens and hells for the sick and dying — and a surreal limbo, in which souls may hover for days, or years, teasing death. But who knows what price we pay for such miracles? Prolonging life, postponing death, we are in the realm of the gods, but our understanding of life and death is hardly godlike.

The longer we talked, the further we strayed from the subject. Invasive procedures, dangerous drugs, the tubes and monitors and scanners of the modern hospital — these aren't just the province of science but of magic, and of politics, since we all bear the costs. So politics came into the discussion, and religion. Of course, it's all politics, if you believe in politics; it's all religion, if you believe in God. Are ghastly birth defects accidental? Do we choose the circumstances of our birth and our death? Thus did we toil, in the stubborn ground of each other's doubts and convictions, digging ourselves into a hole. I called one friend's thinking naive and simplistic; that, she said, sounded just like a man. Soon, we were arguing about our injured feelings. Feelings are bruised, I said, whenever people argue. It's regrettable, but inevitable. All that's inevitable, my wife sighed, is that everyone loses when you argue right and wrong.

Instead of letting the conversation die then, of natural causes, I hovered over it, like a physician with nervous hands. If I had been uncertain, earlier, about the deeper mysteries, I suffered no doubt about the virtues of a good quarrel. An occasional argument seemed to me essential to friendship, to marriage, to democracy itself. If you can't bite, Theodor Reik said, you can't kiss; if you can't curse, you can't bless. The honest force of an argument, I argued, was tonic. A healthy intellectual life was impossible without the heat of vigorous dissent.

The insight moved no one. Indeed, it started us on yet another round. Why, my friend wanted to know, was I being so aggressive? Couldn't I acknowledge the validity of more than one point of view? Not if the other point of view didn't make sense, I insisted. But, my wife said, you have to respect other people's feelings, even when you disagree with their reasoning. Then how, I wanted to know, could you ever argue passionately about anything? Don't we offend the racist's feelings when we speak out against apartheid? Isn't talking with each other, arguing with each other — even offending each other, in the service of truth — more important than the sanctity of feelings?

The more we argued, the more defensive I became. I had staked out the high ground, made my camp on a narrow ledge with truth, but did I want to spend the night up there? To be arguing against the integrity of feelings made no sense to me. Shouldn't I know better than to trust truth more than the wounded look of the woman across from me? The mind creates the abyss, someone has said, and the heart crosses it. What was I making more important than love? I didn't know.

I didn't want to be a bully. I knew better than to insist my experience was more valid than hers. But I was too sullen to acknowledge this. In that dark chamber of my heart, where I confuse being right with being loved, I was reaching for agreement, for approval, like a child reaching for an outstretched hand. To feel hurt because friends disagreed with me — to feel that because they didn't cherish my opinions, they didn't care about me — was absurd, my mind insisted, too absurd to admit.

We said goodbye. Norma and the children went to bed. I sat at the table alone, staring at the immense darkness outside the window, then at my own stubborn face in the glass.

TRAIL'S END

I KNOW I'M IN TROUBLE when Norma starts saving for a tent and sleeping bags. Then she brings home a book with the ominous title *Hiking Trails in North Carolina*. Actually, I'm fond of hiking, especially if I can relax afterward with a bed and a bath. But to my wife, this is like washing down a gourmet dinner with a Dr. Pepper. She wants an experience of nature unmediated by civilized comfort. She wants to show me and Jaime, her thirteen-year-old son, how to rough it.

I've been camping before. But never, she insists, have I experienced the real thing: the thrill of trekking up a mountain toting a full pack, pitching a small tent in the middle of nowhere, no toilet, no shower, no friendly park ranger to answer my dumb questions, just a night sky ablaze with stars, and the hand of nature upon my heart, soothing like a mother.

It's raining when we get to the mountains. We sit in the car hoping to wait it out, but the rain doesn't quit. Finally, we give up and get a room for the night. Jaime says this is his idea of camping: HBO and an indoor pool.

Under clear skies the next morning, I swap nervous, tasteless jokes with Jaime about the dangers that await us. This is, after all, an environmental habitat for bears and cougars; we're packing a snakebite kit; we've brought iodine to decontaminate the water. Since *Mad* is Jaime's favorite magazine, he's a great straight man. But Norma was never a subscriber; she isn't amused by our adolescent humor. Shouldering my frayed canvas backpack, I vow to be serious. I, too, believe in the pioneer virtues, I remind her; this is the same backpack I used when I hitchhiked coast-to-coast twenty years ago, searching for the perfect commune.

But the trail is steeper and muddier than I expected, and I'm surprised how quickly I tire. Hitchhiking on the interstate was less strenuous than laboring up this rocky mountain footpath with nearly fifty pounds on my back. Shoulders aching, legs weary, I soon regret having brought the extra food, the extra clothes, prepared for all emergencies except the most immediate: the bruising weight of my necessities.

Unsure of my footing, vexed that Norma glides along so gracefully under her heavy load, I step gingerly around slick rocks and small puddles. At a sharp turn in the trail, I lose my balance and fall, scraping my knee. Norma asks if I'm all right. I shrug off her question, tell her to be careful. Minutes later, clambering over a sprawl of huge rocks, I lose my balance again, flail desperately for an overhanging branch as Norma and Jaime turn to stare. I suggest we stop to rest.

We ease out of our packs. Around us, nature chatters amiably, the air filled with the stubborn hum of insects, the trilling of birds, the splashing of a nearby stream. Jaime deadpans, "It sounds like one of those meditation tapes."

We hike past stands of birch and oak, dense thickets of rhododendron, waterfalls, brooding cliffs. Finally, about five thousand feet up, in a wooded grove with a dramatic view of the summit, we set up our tents. I'm exhausted and sweaty, and my new boots have given me blisters. But we have to hike farther to fill our canteens from a spring.

I've never been a soldier, but it dawns on me how miserable an infantryman's life must be, even when no one is shooting at you: plodding through mud with a heavy pack plus a weapon and ammunition, day after wearisome day. This is why war is hell, I think. It's like camping, only worse.

The water is supposed to be safe to drink; we add iodine just in case. Then, the sky growing cloudy, we gather kindling for a campfire. But all the dead wood is wet, and our fire hisses indifferently, giving off more smoke than heat. While Norma fans the flames, I boil some water on our one-burner stove, eager for a cup of coffee. The coffee tastes like iodine. Dinner is dehydrated vegetarian chili, which tastes like it sounds. We're barely finished eating when it starts to rain.

I've heard that this mountain has some of the region's most se-
vere weather, that hikers have died here from falls, lightning, and
exposure. What if the wind picks up? What if a tree near us is hit
by lightning? We were warned to get off the mountain during bad
weather, I remind Norma. No, she says, we were warned not to
stand on a ridge during a lightning storm. There's no lightning,
she says, and we're not on a ridge.

The sky turns darker. Jaime crawls into his tent with a book and
a flashlight. Norma settles into her sleeping bag to listen, content-
edly, to the rain. I listen, too. I'm worried about bears, about snakes,
about the weather. I'm worried that if the rain keeps up, our de-
scent will be treacherous, that we'll tumble down the mountain
like boulders in an avalanche. For all the splendor of our surroundings I'm miserable, and inexplicably lonely even with Norma beside
me. Soon, she drifts off to sleep. I want to sleep, too, but our air
mattresses are wafer-thin; the hard ground pummels my aching
body every time I turn. Startled by the smallest sound, I sense
menace everywhere. The night, like an endless hallway, stretches
before me; I try all the doors in the darkness, peering into each
one.

Nature laughs at me. She's an animal with shining teeth, a mother
who doesn't love me. Smoothing her dark skirts, her wild hair blowing free, she asks if I recognize her. No, I murmur, I'm a city boy.
When my wife was learning to love the outdoors — as a Girl Scout,
in the 4-H club, on camping trips with her family — I was learning to love winding boulevards and tall buildings. On darkened
streets, in dingy neighborhoods, I can read the writing on the wall,
but I can't make out nature's wild scrawl. I confuse rustling leaves
with the looming presence of a madman; the smell of black dirt
with the hot, moist breath of a bear.

Large drops of rain hit the tent as the wind picks up. Staring
wide-eyed into the darkness, I remember the words of anthropolo-
gist Richard Nelson. Nature isn't merely created by God, Nelson

writes, nature *is* God. When we walk in the woods we can experience the sacredness with our entire body, breathe it, drink the sacred water as a living communion, touch the living branch. Yet here, in the darkness, on this billion-year-old mountain, it's not God I crave but the safety of home, the way a drowning swimmer craves land. I feel as if I've been stranded in an immense and alien mind I'll never understand, lost in a billion-year-old story in which human history is a footnote.

I have no idea what nature is, I think glumly. I imagine I can apply human qualities to it, as if it were one Big Personality, one seamless something, as if it were an it. Interestingly, those who seem most at home in nature also seem to know it by specifics, not as some transcendent symbol. Maybe Richard Nelson can talk about finding God in nature because he sees the wild world around him in intimate detail, because he watches animals go about their living and dying — in the same way Mother Teresa can talk of seeing God in the face of a starving child.

Is that distant thunder? Nature clearing its throat for some awful announcement? I toss and turn, waiting for daybreak, dismayed at how easily defeated I am by a bad night in the rain. At the first glimmer of light, I wake Norma. Let's skip the coffee, I say, rolling up my sleeping bag. We break camp in silence — Norma knows how unhappy I am; I know she doesn't want to hear about it — and hike down the mountain along a different trail. Descending by switchbacks, then crossing a lush valley, we pass giant ferns, dark ravines, huge fallen trunks covered in moss. It's a scene of unspoiled natural beauty, but my feet are sore, my back aches. I have to concentrate on every step to keep from falling.

Shafts of sunlight illuminate the forest floor, a vision of paradise; I might as well be stuck in traffic, honking my horn. Behind my desk, behind my locked front door, I give thanks for the world. But when the gathering darkness calls to me, I want running water. I want police protection. I want all the wonders of the Industrial Revolution, never mind the cost.

It's a humbling admission. For years, I imagined I could do without civilization: leave it all behind, hitchhike into the wilderness, live without electricity, wear my exile with pride. I never really lived that way, never found the commune, yet I held on to the dream.

In the tent last night, I was reminded that the modern world was created by people just like me, out of their deepest fear and longing; that civilization isn't a mistake someone else keeps making. What would it mean, I ask, to accept my responsibility for it, without excuse or apology, without distancing myself ever so slightly from the poisoned oceans, the acid rain?

We cross a river on broad, flat stones. I hesitate when I come to a crooked, moss-covered rock; Norma, already on the other side, assures me it's safe.

I glance at the swirling water, take a deep breath. What would it mean, I wonder, to stop pretending I've dropped out of the twentieth century, when I'm hurtling with everyone else toward its end?

THE MAN IN THE MIRROR

But the very hairs of your head are all numbered.
Matthew 10 : 30

ON THE BEST OF DAYS, it's a little like falling in love; like opening a stuck window inside yourself; like taking a drug — one that's perfectly legal, dispensed by your own apothecary, your strange and marvelous brain. I don't understand it. I just know I blaze more brightly, my senses keen, my mind and body in communion. Running, I'm a boy again, bolting out the classroom door — not a man behind a desk, a weight upon the world.

I had just returned from a run when a friend dropped by. We sat outside and talked, the air tangy with autumn, the sunlight so bright it seemed to illuminate things from within. When my friend mentioned that her husband was depressed because he'd just turned forty, I said I was surprised. Why did he imagine that getting older was something to be feared?

Surely he didn't believe that middle age was some kind of betrayal? I certainly didn't. At forty-four, I rejoiced in my health, my work, my friends. Time hadn't robbed me of anything, except a few bad habits. I didn't smoke. I'd given up junk food long ago, and I'd cut back on coffee. Most nights, I even got enough sleep. I didn't neglect my emotional health, either: I stayed close to the feelings that made sense and to those that didn't. I ran, but not from myself.

The poet Robert Bly said, when he turned fifty, "I know men who are healthier at fifty than they've ever been before, because a lot of their fear is gone." I, too, felt stronger each year, less burdened with worries and guilt, and my body showed it. How much our bodies reveal, after all — announcing, like billboards, the most intimate things about us: how we insulate ourselves, with a few extra pounds, from the emptiness we don't want to feel; how we keep our shoulders hunched, to ward off the blow that's always coming, but never comes.

Yet my friend's husband knew this, too. He was a thoughtful man, healthy and vigorous. Why would he be deceived by negative images of aging; by the slander of an advertising industry that glorifies youth as a peak experience, compared to which the rest of our life is an inevitable decline we try vainly to delay? In some cultures, older people are venerated, and aging is a sign of maturity and strength. Here, aging is feared, or ridiculed. Think of the jokes we make about birthdays, once our friends are past thirty; the growing apprehension about our looks, our sex appeal; the anxiety about accomplishing something before we get "too old."

I wanted my friend to know my attitude was different. We've been endowed with extraordinary power to shape our lives, I said. Only when we pretend otherwise do we feel powerless, victims of events over which we seem to have no control. Time isn't the enemy; our own limiting beliefs are what age us. If you believe that growing older is tragic, I insisted, you'll grow into a tragic figure, brittle and bitter; if you believe, instead, that the passing years are a celebration of life, who knows what they'll bring?

I went on, in this same vein. These were convictions I'd held for years; they seemed as unarguable as the swaying pines above me, the earth under my feet. Invigorated by my morning run, heartened by the sound of my confident voice, I grinned at my reflection in time's dark river. It was no river of sorrows; not for me.

Yet the very next night, a seemingly inconsequential remark, a bit of good-natured teasing, wiped the grin off my face.

My wife and daughter were in a playful mood, joking with me about my thinning hair. It started out harmlessly. I even joined in the fun. I knew that male baldness follows a distinct pattern: a receding hairline at the temples that one day meets the thinning spot at the crown. But I wasn't worried. When I looked in the mirror, I still saw plenty of dark curls, a little rumpled and unmanageable, like me. Occasionally, I'd see myself from an angle that was less flattering, but what difference did it make? To be vibrantly alive meant staying honest and undefended about such changes. Besides, I was a long way from being *bald*.

Not according to my wife and daughter. My conceit, their merry eyes seemed to say, was even more amusing than my thinning hair. I told them to stop teasing, but they danced around my objections, too giddy to hear the warning in my voice. "Look," Norma said, peering at my hairline, then at the thinning spot on top, "the two bald spots are meeting!" Mara laughed.

If a howling wind had suddenly slapped me in the face, I wouldn't have been more stunned. I turned toward Norma, disbelieving.

"No, they're not," I said.

"Yes, they are."

"You're exaggerating," I insisted. Norma just smiled. Her tender gaze — the patient look she gives me when she knows I'm fooling myself — was worse than the teasing. I turned away.

Sullenly, I told Mara to go to her room. Norma looked at me in surprise. I stared back at her, my eyes two boarded-up windows; nobody home. Dimly, I knew she hadn't meant to hurt me. She didn't know — until that night, I didn't know — how painful a subject this was. Hadn't I just boasted that time wasn't the enemy? Yet time — unimpressed by my little speech, indifferent to my unarguable convictions — was beckoning me toward the uncertain future, and I didn't want to go.

Too late, Norma tried to change the subject, but I wouldn't talk to her the rest of the evening. When we got into bed, I was still feeling angry. I refused to get under the covers; I didn't want our bodies even accidentally to touch. So I lay there shivering as the night grew colder, staring wide-eyed at the ceiling, unable to sleep. Images assailed me. I saw, as if they were long-lost friends, my bald spot and my receding hairline meeting, reaching across the years of my life to shake hands. I imagined how I'd look in a few years, a balding man trying desperately to deny what's obvious, parting my hair at my ear, swooping it over my head. I'd face the mirror each morning with a soldierly smile, remembering better days. Oh time, that barber that goes on cutting, oblivious to your plea to take just a little off the sides, leave a little more on top. Time, come to remind me that all the health food and jogging and honesty about my feelings meant nothing to him, a sprig of parsley on the feast of me. Oh, he would feast on me. . . .

I curled up on my side of the bed, as far from Norma as I could get. She was the messenger whose message I wanted to deny but couldn't, so I denied her instead.

The next day, I spent longer than usual in front of the mirror. The last time I'd studied myself this carefully was when I was an adolescent, and had started *growing* hair: pubic hair; hair under my arms; hair on my upper lip and on my chin; and those first few chest hairs, like the first rays of dawn streaking across the horizon, heralding my manhood. How amazing, at twelve or thirteen, to watch myself turn into someone else. It was all there, hair in all the right places — and on my head, of course, more hair than I knew what to do with, hair I took for granted even as I fought its unruly curliness. I'd rub some hair cream on my scalp; then, with merciless brushing, I'd struggle to get the wave in front just right. Some mornings, I'd spend fifteen minutes in front of the mirror, coaxing that wave into place.

After all these years, was I still so concerned about my appearance? Hadn't I strived to go beyond appearances? I examined myself now from every angle. Of course I cared how I looked! My studied nonchalance about my appearance — the rumpled clothes, the bushy beard, the wire-rimmed glasses — *was* my look. Losing my hair threatened my self-image as profoundly as a sudden breeze on my way to school thirty years ago could undo fifteen minutes of careful brushing and ruin my day.

I drew my chin against my chest and leaned forward, straining to see the top of my scalp. I wanted to prove to myself that Norma was exaggerating, but the closer I looked, the less hair I saw. Oh my hair — hair that once fell past my shoulders. For seven years, back when long hair stood for something, I didn't cut it. Dark and tangled, it was my declaration of independence, my way of keeping faith with myself, banner of my gypsy soul. When I finally did cut it, because long hair no longer stood for anything, it was still a symbol of distinction — proving that I could be myself *without* needing to look different. What did my hair say about me now? That I was a middle-aged man, balding and vain?

On the street, instead of noticing laughing children or beautiful women, I started noticing balding men: I noticed whether they were more or less bald than I. Ram Dass once observed that we put people into three categories: those who are makable; those who are competition for the ones who are makable; and those who are irrelevant. I was no longer on the make, I brooded, but I still liked to think of myself as someone whose seasoned looks appealed to women. Yet without my curly hair, would I still be the kind of man women flirted with, or treated instead with *respect*? I didn't want to be like the bald men on television — the safe, non-threatening type. Married, and a father, I was in no hurry to become a father *figure*.

A well-dressed couple caught my eye. The man was about my age, the slender woman much younger. She was laughing at something he'd said. He winked. She smiled at him adoringly. Deeply tanned, with a trim, peppery beard, he was strikingly handsome, despite being almost totally bald. I felt momentarily comforted, like the victim of a natural disaster who discovers a fellow survivor.

I went to the public library. With a sheepish smile at the woman behind the desk, I checked out some books on the subject. Then, hoping I wouldn't run into anyone I knew, I hurried to my car — as embarrassed as if I'd just stepped out of a video store with a couple of X-rated films under my arm.

Alas, scientists seemed to know as little about baldness as porno directors do about sex. Why some men and not others lose their hair is an enigma. It has something to do with heredity, something to do with male sex hormones, though the exact cause-and-effect relationship is hardly understood. The overproduction of sex hormones might be responsible; far from indicating a lack of masculinity, losing one's hair might result from an excess of it. This theory appealed to me.

But for all their theories, scientists don't have a clue what to do about baldness. For men willing to pay thousands of dollars and undergo a series of sometimes painful operations, hair transplants are available. Others wear wigs. (I couldn't picture myself wearing a wig; I never even wear a *hat*.) Regrettably, few of the remedies on the market are effective; the search for a cure has turned up one worthless potion after another.

But I'm not someone who puts immense faith in science. I believe in the power of the mind, in the innate ability of the body to heal itself. Many ailments can be affected by a change in consciousness; physical degeneration can be reversed. Might it not be possible, I wondered — through visualization, for example, or a change in diet — to keep myself from becoming more bald, or even to grow back the hair I'd lost? No one really knows why the cells stop producing hair, any more than they understand why, in cancer patients, the cells multiply so shamelessly. Yet some cancer patients are able to stimulate their immune systems by picturing their white blood cells as knights on horseback attacking the cancer. Less dramatically, I've used visualization techniques many times to ward off colds, to evoke feelings of well-being and strength. If I was so certain that we fashion our own reality — that our deepest beliefs determine what we see and don't see, what we do and don't call real — why not visualize a body that's healthy and beautiful?

But when would it stop? Would I try to resist other signs of aging, too, as if aging itself were a disease, an insult to the spirit? Would I try to keep my skin from growing more wrinkled? My beard from turning more gray? If I viewed every physical change as an intolerable loss, wasn't I denying reality itself, and the inevitability of change? When did natural healing become unnatural? Besides, I wondered, what would be worse: losing my hair, or spending twenty minutes every morning praying not for world peace, or for the salvation of my soul, but for my looks never to fade?

Perhaps I was worried that Norma would no longer find me attractive. After all, I'm ten years older than she is. Suddenly, that seemed important. I was at the mercy of a body that had shown every sign until now of lasting forever, as I imagined our passion would last, not die out slowly, its ghost moving through us when we embraced, haunting us with memories of better days. How improbable that seemed — yet how improbable to be starting the week this way, glum-faced and uncertain. How improbable to see, in time's dark river, an old man staring back at me — a man who looked just like me, except with less hair and more wrinkles; a man who called himself Sy yet was clearly an impostor, no longer able to get up before dawn each morning or run three miles or do fifty push-ups or make love with his wife for hours. . . .

Yet time was calling to Norma, too, running his hand across her face, touching her hair with the tint of our mortality. So what if I didn't have the same body as when I married her? We all change. Relinquishing a self-image that was no longer real shouldn't be so hard. How many former selves had I left behind? The small boy, the awkward teenager — they were gone, as surely as spring is gone by summer and summer by fall. The young journalist who believed the facts would save us, the young poet who believed love would — gone, too, like leaves driven by a scattering wind. How many once-familiar faces and places I barely remembered, as if they were someone else's memories. But we all go that way: memory, like youth, fades, until what lies behind us is nearly as unknown as what lies ahead.

How unkind I'd been to Norma, I thought miserably. How unbearably glib I must have sounded to my friend.

That night, Norma apologized for having hurt my feelings. I was sorry, too, I said, for having acted the way I did. I reached for her, drew her to me. I wanted the taste of her, her body pressed against me — the way the future presses against the present, the present against the past. Here and now, I wanted nothing but us between us, our lovemaking as passionate as ever, and it was — or so I assured myself, as we drifted off to sleep, Norma's arms around me, my face buried in her hair.

But I woke up the next morning still confused. I felt as if I'd wandered into some foreign city, not on any map — some old neighborhood, some walled-in part of me, a place of immeasurable grief.

I remembered something my friend David once said: "I always knew I was going to die. I just didn't think I'd get old."

For someone who knew that aging was nothing to fear, my beliefs fit me now like a bad suit. Time had called to me and I'd come running, ready to beg for my life, for a few hairs on my head. In the face of my own suddenly indisputable mortality, what I knew was suddenly insubstantial, smoke up the chimney: gone, like wisps, my hair, my beliefs.

I'd always scorned the notion of a midlife crisis. Setting off, in middle age, on a compulsive quest for lost youth, or a fervent search for inner validation, seemed, in fact, a bit bourgeois. Some anxiety about growing older was probably universal, but quitting a job in mid-career, trading in the station wagon for a sports car, becoming suddenly suspicious of the counterfeit luxury one had spent a lifetime acquiring and defending — these were the prerogatives of the well-to-do. A midlife crisis was just one more aspect of mainstream culture I'd planned to avoid, the way I'd avoided selling my soul to a corporation.

Yet, right on schedule, I was changing, too — no matter that my lifestyle was different from that of the man next door, who wore a tie every day and voted Republican. I began to realize that what I'd really hoped to avoid wasn't just becoming middle-class but becoming middle-aged — as if, by escaping one, I might escape the other; as if my values made me immune to the coarse demands, the disagreeable consequences, of growing old.

When I was a boy, my grandmother would reminisce about how beautiful she'd been as a young woman; how her arthritic, crippled legs had once been so shapely; how men would turn and look as she walked by. In her wedding photograph — with her proud posture, her black hair framing her unlined face — she looked so different from the wrinkled, bent, gray-haired woman before me. That someone could change so dramatically made sense to me only in the most abstract way. I accepted it, the way I accepted many things in my young life. But I had no idea what it meant.

As a grown man, do I understand it any better? "We dance 'round in a ring and suppose," wrote Robert Frost. "But the secret sits in the middle and knows." By facing my anxieties about growing older, I was hoping to get closer to the secret, but mostly I've gotten closer to my fears. They're like sleeping dogs: wake one, you rouse the others. After all, it's not just my hair I'm losing. My memory isn't as good as it used to be; nor, as the cold weather reminds me, is the circulation in my fingers and toes. Nor is sex the demon, or the refuge, it once was; the urge is there, as insistent as ever when it's there, but there are days, amazingly, when I hardly feel the urge at all.

I wanted to end this on a note of acceptance, suggesting that losing my hair was a kind of blessing — a benign but persuasive reminder not to take my life for granted. But most of the time I don't experience it that way. Instead, I project my worst fears on the future. I conspire with the mirror to hide my real self behind my face. To pretend to be more accepting would be like putting on a wig.

No less blatantly than those who try to deny death with spas and cosmetics and surgeons, I, too, make death the enemy, and try to defend myself against it — with the myth of my ever-increasing vigor, with innumerable little lies. Immediate reminders of my mortality are few. It's easy, living where I do, to pretend death is slightly unreal: on my street no one is dying of malnutrition, or disease, or war. Death happens out of sight. It's the real X-rated scene, the one few of us can bear.

I've known moments of transcendence — ecstatic experiences that have shown me death is nothing to fear. But, like distant islands in a vast sea, these moments can seem remote, inaccessible. Most of the time I cling to this weathered lifeboat, this body, and don't like being reminded it wasn't built to last.

OF THE BRAVE

I WAS DRIVING HOME from a visit with a friend, thinking about getting some ice cream, and fighting the usual battle in my head about using sweets to comfort myself. I was thinking about my friend, and about the war with Iraq. A ground war was imminent, the radio said.

I drove past the bars and restaurants on West Rosemary Street, past the old yellow house where *The Sun* office used to be. I'm fond of this neighborhood — Chapel Hill's low-rent district, its rumpled back porch — with its cheerfully seedy, vaguely bohemian air. It's especially lovely in spring, which comes early to Chapel Hill — a reckless lover who sends flowers in February, impatient for winter to end.

At Internationalist Books, the lights were still on. I considered stopping, knowing I could count on a friendly hello from Bob Sheldon, the owner. More than a bookseller, Bob was a fervent political organizer, a sixties radical who had stayed true to his convictions.

I'd see Bob often in the parking lot between our buildings. (Before we moved the office, I used to joke that the Internationalist — its shelves filled with books on Marxist theory, Palestinian rights, feminist and gay and lesbian issues, Green politics, black nationalism — was just to the left of *The Sun*.) I might be reading manuscripts on the stoop when he'd arrive on his motorcycle, his strawberry-blond, shoulder-length hair streaming behind him. Because Bob didn't open the store until nearly midday, parcels addressed to the Internationalist were frequently left with us. The UPS driver would grumble about Bob's "banker's hours." He was convinced that people like Bob and I didn't know what hard work was. I'd smile, having been up half the night putting together an issue. I knew that Bob, who supported himself with another job, was no less devoted.

I don't know how many books Bob sold. Plenty of people came to the store just to browse through magazines or get into a discussion. Bob loved to talk politics. A conscientious objector during

the Vietnam War, he used to distribute Revolutionary Communist Party literature on local campuses, and was once fired from a
textile mill for his unionizing activities. Yet Bob defied easy labels.
A streetwise intellectual, he danced to reggae, worked as a regis-
tered nurse, and was a former jock with letters in wrestling, track,
and football. Even among dissenters, he was a dissenter. While he
refused to embrace nonviolence — insisting that if you lived in
Guatemala or South Africa you might have no choice but to be
violent — he was a gentle, soft-spoken man with a keen sense of
humor; no matter how serious the conversation, there were always
some laughs.

If I had stopped that night, we might have talked about the
Gulf War, which Bob emphatically opposed. I might have kidded
him about being a celebrity: a few weeks earlier, he'd been interviewed on local television, and he was now the best-known anti-war
activist in town. I might have picked through the Central American handicrafts or the international music cassettes. If I had stopped
that night — as U.S. planes dropped bombs on Iraq, and Democrats cowered in their bunkers, and Republicans paraded behind
the flag, and something shadowy and menacing, some twisted
dream of glory, loped again across the land — I might have gotten
to see Bob Sheldon one last time.

Bob's friend Ken was supposed to meet him at the Internationalist around nine that night. But when Ken opened the creaky
screen door, he found Bob sprawled on the floor, bleeding and
unconscious. He'd been shot in the head. Bob was rushed to the
hospital, but he never regained consciousness. He died the following day.

The bullet came from a small-caliber weapon, fired from less
than ten feet away. There was no sign of a struggle, no immediate
indication that the store had been robbed, nor was Bob known to
have any personal enemies. The immediate speculation was that
Bob was killed because of his political beliefs. The timing of his

death was too significant to ignore; his television appearance must have angered many viewers. This is North Carolina, after all, which keeps reelecting Jesse Helms to the Senate. This is the state where, not too many years ago, Klansmen shot and killed members of the Communist Workers Party and were never convicted. A friend said, "Bob stood in harm's way. He knew that. He'd been threatened before, and he didn't move. This was the first bullet fired in the ground war."

Others suggest that West Rosemary Street was too busy, even in the evening, for an assassination. And, despite initial reports that no money was taken from the store, it turns out that Bob kept two cash boxes; one appeared to be missing. But Bob's friends doubt it was a robbery; they say he was savvy enough to have handled a holdup without being killed, that he wouldn't have fought over money. Besides, armed robberies are rare in this town, murders even more rare; and anybody looking for cash on West Rosemary Street could easily have found a better target.

As I write this, police have no suspects and have made no arrests.

Several days after the shooting, nearly five hundred people packed a local church to mourn Bob's death. One woman told how Bob had offered her money at a dance after her wallet was stolen. They were virtual strangers, she said, and she was hesitant to take it. Bob said, "I know you'll do the same for someone else."

Marilyn, with whom Bob had lived for many years, said that about a week after she and Bob separated, their cat Max died. "Bob had Max for a very long time; he loved him. He took him to the vet, and they said Max wasn't in pain, but that he was dying. So Bob put him in a box and stayed with him. I remember Bob saying he didn't think anyone should have to die alone."

One person called Bob "the most combative socialist" she'd ever known. Another referred, jokingly, to his "rabid, testosterone-laden diatribes."

Dan, a fellow activist, later said, "Though I was sometimes put off by his sectarian terminology, I could always respect his commitment and sincerity." Even in applying for a credit card, Dan said, Bob wanted to know how to get the politically correct Working Assets card. "I kidded him about becoming bourgeois — a yuppie Marxist — and he laughed at himself, something Bob did often."

I didn't always agree with Bob either. I suspect that, like many radicals, he sought from politics what others just as unrealistically seek from religion: a kind of paradise on earth. Yet I respected him enormously. He created not just a bookstore, but a meeting place for local activists, a community hub where people could question and challenge each other and the culture at large.

Bob understood what it meant to turn a stand into a life, by turns thrilling and boring. He lived his revolution, not as if it were something outside himself, something impossibly distant, but here and now, as real as bills to be paid, books shelved, coffee cups rinsed. He believed what he was taught as a child about freedom and justice, and this made him dangerous. Of course, democracy itself is dangerous to those who think society is supposed to run with all the quiet efficiency of an expensive foreign car. Democracy is raucous and uncomfortable — an old jalopy with bent fenders, a shirt that's never ironed, hair that's never combed, a busy Saturday when there are always too many errands to do, too many injustices to protest, never enough time.

"Every revolution evaporates," said Kafka, "leaving behind only the slime of a new bureaucracy." This is true not only of governments, but of individuals: the moment of realization, of inspiration, becomes institutionalized, trivialized. One reason I admired Bob so much is that he kept the revolution alive inside himself.

I don't know what war Bob died in. Maybe he was the first casualty in the ground war with Iraq. Or maybe it was the war of the cities — rich against poor, poor against poor, neighborhood against neighborhood, with casualties measured in robberies and muggings and rapes.

Even if the murderer is arrested, his or her motivation laid bare, in some sense Bob's death will remain a mystery. With all our psychological insight, do we really know why people do what they do? Why they love each other and murder each other? Why marriages, and nations, turn sour? Why the same type of misfortune cripples one person and brings out the best in another? Do we know why one man, watching Bob being interviewed on TV, might mutter something under his breath and reach for a beer — while another man, embittered by failure, convinced of his own powerlessness, might reach instead for a gun?

His death reminds me that nothing keeps us here: not our commitment or our fear of commitment; not the words we've written or the words we haven't written; not the fear of dying, either, or laughing at the fear — as if death were a joke, as if you could tell the joke again and again, never getting to the punch line.

All our lives are tragic, James Baldwin writes, "simply because the earth turns and the sun inexorably rises and sets, and one day, for each of us, the sun will go down for the last, last time. Perhaps the whole root of our trouble, the human trouble, is that we will sacrifice all the beauty of our lives, will imprison ourselves in totems, taboos, crosses, blood sacrifices, steeples, mosques, races, armies, flags, nations, in order to deny the fact of death, which is the only fact we have."

How we struggle to understand! Every day, it seems, a new book arrives on my desk explaining how we create our own reality, how everything is some kind of karmic unfolding, how we're each like characters in a novel we ourselves have written, living out a tale intricate and beautiful and strange. Yet these ideas that explain so much, these ideas that celebrate the endless coupling of mystery and meaning, are born of a deeper mystery we can never comprehend. Psychology, philosophy, spirituality — they're like games we invent, with cards we don't know the meaning of, and so we try to compensate for our ignorance by devising ever more elaborate rules of play. We confuse facts with truth, honesty with understanding, stories about reality with reality itself.

Meanwhile, someone puts a gun to your head. They want money. They want you not to be who you are. America puts a gun to the head of the world, pulls the trigger, insists it was self-defense.

The Sky's the Limit

THE SAME DAY I get the bad news about my gums, I find out the hole in the ozone layer is worse than anyone thought.

It's not just that the hole is getting bigger. We're eggs on the griddle: higher doses of ultraviolet radiation leaking through the fragile ozone shield mean more skin cancers, more cataracts, you name it. But now, scientists report that in the Antarctic, where the hole in the ozone layer was discovered, there's been a 12 percent decline in the growth of phytoplankton, the tiny, single-cell plants that are eaten by nearly all aquatic animals. According to one researcher, the effect eventually "could cascade through the food chain."

I read the story to Norma, who shakes her head. What's more, she says, those tiny, single-cell plants produce more oxygen than the rain forest. I nod. The ozone layer, the greenhouse effect, acid rain: I get them mixed up. I took biology when it was the study of life, not disaster; when "the sky is falling" was a line in a children's story, not a headline. Maybe I'd understand more about the environment if I cared more. I tell myself it's people I care about: crowded, brawling cities; politics; literature; the life of the mind. I joke, like Woody Allen, about my "twoness" with nature. Norma doesn't laugh. She understands more, she worries more, about the environment. I worry what to say about it. "None of this is funny," Norma says. I sigh. "I thought you liked Woody Allen."

The dentist shakes her head. The tenderness in the gums, she says, the slight bleeding — most people consider these symptoms a normal sign of aging. They're not. They're a sign of sickness. Invisible and painless in its early stages, the disease is easy to ignore even as bacteria attack the gum tissue. Later, after the bones and ligaments that support the teeth have been damaged, after the foul breath and oozing pus, after the disease has turned into something called periodontitis, surgery may be required; tooth loss is inevitable.

Periodontitis: a word that sends you to your knees, begging for forgiveness. A word that dresses in black and smells of disinfectant. The dentists must have stayed up all night, tossing words back and forth like frisbees, before they came up with this one. If we were told the world had periodontitis, wouldn't we be more alarmed? Words, I tell Norma, are everything. The environmentalists need to learn this. Their metaphors are too bland, too agreeable. On a chilly day, global warming sounds friendly, like curling up before a fire. The greenhouse effect? I think of ferns.

I picture the planet on the dentist's chair, getting the awful news. *Periodontitis?* The planet gulps. *It can't be that bad.* The pockets around some of the teeth are pretty deep, the dentist says. *We meant to floss.* Of course, the dentist says. *We'll start tonight.* Tonight, the dentist says. Like a priest who has listened to too many confessions, she smiles tenderly, wearily. She calls this the pleading stage. She knows that we're wedded to catastrophe, that we'd sooner argue over our epitaph than change our habits.

Not me. No more jokes about recycled toilet paper, I promise Norma. I'm on my knees.

That night I floss. I brush. I read *A Healthier Mouth: It's Up To You.* I floss again. I think, maybe we're not more alarmed because the hole in the ozone layer isn't a problem for most of us — the way the economy is a problem, or the car's run-down battery is a problem, or, let's face it, what to have for lunch is a problem. The ozone layer is remote, twenty miles up in the stratosphere: about as far away as the ice skating rink in Hillsborough, where my fifteen-year-old daughter asked me to drive her the other night. Get a ride with someone else, I said. But how I worried when she was late.

Yet what good is worrying, or pointing a finger? The newspaper says ozone depletion today is the result of emissions from thirty years ago. But thirty years ago I'd never heard of fluorocarbons or flossing. So who's to blame? Marilyn Monroe for using spray deodorant? John F. Kennedy for not putting a stop to it? We may as well blame our love affair with America, her tall buildings and long highways, her industrial sleek and shine. Or God, for giving us all this freedom, with only one stipulation, one tiny, nagging clause in the otherwise perfect contract: that we learn what freedom really means.

I work the floss along the curved surface of each tooth, like a shoeshine boy with his buffing rag. I floss carefully, because plaque is sticky, practically invisible, clinging to tooth surfaces as tenaciously as Exxon to its profits, oil to a dead bird's wing. I floss because I want to clean up the toxic dump I've made of my mouth. I floss because, as Wendell Berry says, one person who changes his ways is worth a hundred who talk about it.

Standing before the mirror, eighteen inches of nylon thread wrapped too tightly around my fingers, my mouth oozing blood, do I really imagine I'm healing the planet? Individual gestures are important, but why sentimentalize the power of the individual, as if each of us could be a Gandhi or a Mother Teresa? This is Earth Day rhetoric, nailing us to the wall while the real criminals slip away.

I swing between hope and despair on the vine of each day's headlines. I mutter helplessly about America as if it were something I accidentally stepped in. Still, every choice has implications I can barely imagine: walking to the store instead of driving, or boycotting a certain product, or growing some tomatoes, or marching in a demonstration, or demonstrating what it means to govern myself. The body, too, calls out for compassion; it doesn't want to be treated the way the polluters treat the rivers and the skies. Is my body mine, to do with as I please? Is it private property? After all, oneness isn't a lofty idea, something abstract and spiritual, but a bare-bones description of reality, spun of individual acts.

Sometimes what matters is changing a habit. The only way I'm going to make flossing a daily routine — I know, because I've tried before and failed — is to floss right after dinner, instead of waiting until bedtime when I'm tired. But this means not snacking after dinner, not turning to food as consolation for sadness or boredom.

Sometimes what matters is paying attention to my resolve, which turns on itself, analyzes and mocks itself: does the world depend on people like *me*? What a struggle to be present, completely present, with the dying oceans and the dying trees, with this mortal body on this mortal planet.

We had the recyling bins outside the office for months before I started separating my trash at the end of the day. It was too much trouble to sift through my wastebasket, separating the white paper from the yellow paper from the catalogs from the cardboard. From the apple cores. From the plastic container still sticky with cottage cheese. Who wanted to stand outside, in the cold, in the heat, picking through the detritus of the day? It was like flossing. I liked it better when healing the planet meant long hair and rock music and marching against the war, when it meant telling everyone else what needed to be changed.

REFRAIN

I DIDN'T UNDERSTAND what he meant when I first heard John Lennon sing, "No one can harm you. Feel your own pain." But I knew his words were true, just as a sudden change in the weather is true, just as the alarm clock with its shrill ring is true.

Over the years, Lennon's words have become a kind of koan for me, simple yet perplexing, speaking to my stunning forgetfulness, my odd amnesia about my emotional life. I needed such a reminder recently, and it arrived right on time, with an emphasis hardly less dramatic than if Lennon himself had appeared before me, radiant and ghostly.

It was a wet spring day, and the rain had finally stopped falling. I was out running, feeling dark and sullen despite the fleecy clouds and flowering dogwoods, brooding about the argument I'd had earlier that week with my wife. I'd overheard her joking with another woman about some man, the kind of benign innuendo I knew wasn't really threatening — except, alas, to me. It's as difficult for me to trust her, or anyone, as it is for me to admit it — unless I veil my distrust with cleverness, or, if I'm really threatened, with an argument that lasts for days.

It was the kind of argument that called forth the child in me, called to him the way a child is called from sleep. He came into the room, groggy, uncertain, needing reassurance. But he was ignored: by my wife, because I wouldn't tell her he was there; by me, because I wouldn't acknowledge he existed.

Mostly, I argued with myself. Since Norma insisted her remark was innocent, and I was unable to prove otherwise — or to be honest with her about the depth of my fear — I sulked. I didn't address my real heartache: that, as a child, I'd felt betrayed again and again; that I'd learned to deny my pain, to betray *myself*, like an animal, caught in a trap, chewing off its leg to escape; that I still betray myself by ignoring my feelings, and thus fear betrayal by others in countless, subtle ways.

Past shops, past houses, past bleary-eyed students on their way to class, I ran, running again over the argument. Climbing a hill, I lengthened my stride, legs pumping, the beat of my feet on the pavement a counterpoint to the voices in my head. The rhythm of my body was familiar, predictable, and so were the voices, a chorus of discontent. I blamed Norma for her feelings. I blamed myself for mine. Yet, as I reached the crown of the hill, sweat pouring down my face and body, there was another voice, cutting through the din of accusation: John Lennon's voice, with its old refrain, reminding me not to steal my own heart away, then pine for myself. *No one can harm you*, my blood sang. *Feel your own pain.*

After all these years, why couldn't I remember? Why did I still believe that others could harm or save me? What lies we tell ourselves. Abandoned once, we abandon ourselves again and again.

I looked around at the wet flowers, the weeping blossoms. What a beautiful morning, yet how untouched by beauty I felt. What do I ever see, I thought bitterly, but the images I create?

I pictured myself in a darkened theater, watching a movie I'd written and directed, and seen countless times. The projector whirred away, throwing images on the screen. The projector was my judging mind; the lens that distorted everything, my unacknowledged pain. Small wonder that everyone I saw — my friends, my children, my wife — was an illusion. There I was, too, a bad actor with lousy lines.

I kept running. My breathing deepened as I settled into a steadier pace. I knew I had a choice: to suffer the images or to face the pain. To stop projecting onto others is difficult but freeing: the kind of freedom Lennon sang about; the freedom of remembering there's no protection — and none needed — against life.

To experience others this way, I thought, to stop projecting, to step into the light from that dark and gloomy place — what grace! It was an amazing thought, not because it had never occurred to me, but because this time something in me rose to greet it. Mercy's wing had swept me up. I felt lighter; the world hummed with a different possibility. Joy traveled through me like a wave. Was it the endorphins — a runner's high — or some divine benevolence, and who's to say they're not the same? I picked up the pace, heart and mind joined in a rare unity, as I cut across the street.

If my eye hadn't been fixed on glory, I might have noticed the light. But I didn't even see the car until I heard the frantic horn and the squealing brakes — and by then it was too late. I caught a glimpse of it just before it hit me. Terror bloomed in me, a primal *Oh no* that never escaped my lips. My mind was unable to make the leap my body did, as I bounced off the hood and was sent sprawling to the street.

I hit the pavement. Time rushed back in, like the soul to the body after a dream. Terror gave way to wonder as I realized, incredulously, I was unharmed. I'd had the wind knocked out of me, and I was bruised. But there were no broken bones, no blood, no real injuries.

The driver jumped out, his face as ashen as mine must have been, his voice tremulous. "Are you OK?" "Yes," I said, getting up unsteadily. "Yes. I think I'm fine." A policeman hurried over. He looked me up and down. "Do you need to go to the hospital?" I assured him I was all right.

The driver said he hadn't seen me until I was in front of him. Fortunately, he said, he was slowing down to make a turn. I was sorry, I said. I wanted him to know I didn't blame him. Actually, I felt surprisingly tender toward him, our lives for this moment oddly entwined. I reached out to touch his arm. "This is a lucky day for both of us," I suggested. He nodded grimly. "I'm just glad," he said, "that you're alive."

Rejoice, rejoice. Not to put too fine a point on it, so was I. I'd been hit by a car, yet I was walking away unharmed. Mercy's wing had swept me up, and put me down. How strange that earlier that week, a few words I didn't want to hear had hurt me so much more.

HOME IS WHERE

ALWAYS TOOK PRIDE in the places I lived, rundown as they were: the small room in a garage, just big enough for a bed and a desk, where I typed up the first issues of *The Sun*; the dilapidated old house in the country, with high ceilings and no heat, which I shared with six friends and uncounted dogs and cats; a mattress in the back of the office, when I couldn't afford a place of my own.

Having once lived for a year in a van, I knew what the real luxuries were: a bed to sleep on, a light to read by, a roof to keep me dry. I liked beautiful things, but I understood the difference between living elegantly and living expensively. I could create a mood with hand-me-downs and thrift-shop finds, draping a scarf over a window, watching sunlight decorate a room as it moved from the chair to the bed to my loved one's sleeping face.

Like my shoulder-length hair, my frayed jeans, my beat-up car, these ramshackle surroundings said something about me. Perhaps I romanticized my small sacrifices, prided myself on living simply. But since I had chosen this way of life, I didn't think of myself as a victim. I didn't really mind the drafty rooms, the chipped and peeling paint, the pipes that froze in winter. Forgoing middle-class luxuries was, I believed, as political an act as pulling the lever in a voting booth or marching in a demonstration.

Even after I got a different car, bought new jeans, trimmed my hair, I didn't give up my allegiance to unpretentious surroundings. Not until three years ago, when I moved to a split-level house in the suburbs.

Norma and I didn't want to leave our cabin deep in the woods, at the end of a dirt road, far from cars and neighbors. But after years of being separated from my children, I was about to become a full-time parent again; my daughters, both of them nearly teenagers, were coming to live with me, and we needed a bigger place, closer to town.

I didn't want to live in a neighborhood where the developer had cut down all the trees then named the neighborhood after them;

where the houses weren't just homes but temples to the *idea* of home, places of worship where material success could be endlessly revered. Frank Lloyd Wright said he could design a house that would make a married couple get a divorce; to my mind, most houses already kept us divorced from our bodies, from the world around us, from the invisible bonds that make community real.

We ended up in a subdevelopment where they left the trees but named the streets after Revolutionary War battles. Lurking behind the neat lawns and mock colonial facades were, I was sure, enough votes to put George Bush in the White House that year. I'd be about as welcome here as crab grass. Still, in a world where home can be anything — a refugee tent, an abandoned car — I hated to complain. I wanted the inward and outward parts of my life to reflect each other, to say something about my integrity, my commitment to social change. But I also wanted my daughters to be safe and comfortable. I used to think that living somewhere "for the kids" was hypocritical. "When children appear," Chekhov wrote, "we justify all our weaknesses, compromises, snobberies, by saying, 'It's for the children's sake.'" Yet was it right to insist that my children see the world as I did — actively resisting a culture they barely understood, living out *my* version of an authentic life? After all, so many of my ideas seemed quaint to them, less an expression of my vaulted integrity than of my idiosyncratic personality. They knew my disdain for middle-class respectability was riddled with contradictions; that I'd always been an outsider; that I'd probably feel estranged even in the most politically-correct part of town.

It took a long time to get used to being here. On our first night, I lay awake, listening to the unfamiliar sounds of the house settling back on its haunches. Outside, the tall pines swayed and whispered. Downstairs, the refrigerator hummed. I closed my eyes and started to drift off when, suddenly, the ice-maker coughed and I jumped: I'd never had a refrigerator that made ice.

We got rid of the shiny fixtures and fancy drapes, unpacked our books and albums and Indian fabrics. I wanted to transform the

place immediately, make it ours — but the house stubbornly re-
sisted. We argued endlessly about how to make the rooms more
inviting, but no matter what we tried it was still a split-level house
in the suburbs. Norma said it would take months, maybe years,
for the house to feel like home. I sulked in a corner, staring dole-
fully at the fake-wood paneling.

The paneling is still there, but I don't notice it. (Does a house
become home when you accept its imperfections?) These days, I'll
even admit to liking the neighborhood. People walk a great deal
— before going to work, after getting home from work — as if
walking itself were their work, so assiduously do they walk. Cars
drive slowly. Children ride their bikes. The people who live here,
I've found out, aren't all Republicans, and they certainly aren't my
enemies. If their struggle to raise families and make ends meet
seems more banal than heroic, if their fears and dreams seem less
vivid than my own, perhaps that's because they're still fictions to
me, not real people; not my enemies, but not my friends.

Will I ever make friends here? There's barely enough time for
the friends I have, and there are so many other things I want to do:
write more, spend more time with my children, work an afternoon
a week at the shelter for the homeless. But I'm too busy. I barely
have time to read the newspaper.

So it was by chance that I came across a story a few weeks ago
about one of my neighbors. I discovered he grew up in New York
City, which may explain the affinity I felt when I first saw him. Or
maybe it was the graying beard, the wire-rimmed glasses, something about the eyes. He looked like a kindred spirit, I thought,
my kind of guy. Then, immediately, I corrected myself. Who was I
kidding? In this neighborhood? He smiled and I smiled back. In
the three years since, we've never spoken a word to each other.

According to the story, my neighbor, an engineer who retired
after twenty years in the military, had been given an award for
public service. He builds houses for low-income people through
Habitat for Humanity; shows up before dawn at the community

NATIVE TONGUE

IT WAS SUPPOSED to be a romantic night without the children. But the motel walls were so thin, we could hear the elderly couple in the next room talking and playing cards until nearly midnight, their voices — very Southern, very proper — looping around our whispered endearments and labored breathing. Since we could only wonder what *they* were hearing, we became a bit self-conscious, as if our parents were in the next room. This was amusing, but not for long, and about as romantic as balancing the checkbook.

At least the view from our window wasn't disappointing. When the sun nudged us awake the next morning, we could see a blue lake and a lot of blue sky and the twin mountains of Flat Top and Sharp Top, known in this part of Virginia as the Peaks of Otter, looming majestically in the pale light.

Sharp Top looked like the kind of mountain a child might draw, rising abruptly to a pointed peak. There were higher mountains nearby, according to our brochure, but none as intriguing. No one was sure how the Peaks of Otter got their picturesque name. Native Americans had hunted elk, deer, and bear here, but historians were certain there had never been otters. Perhaps the colonists who settled the area named the Peaks after fondly remembered mountains in their native Scotland.

I'd learned enough for one morning, but Norma kept reading. We could hike to the summit of Sharp Top, she said, along a rugged, winding path that was strenuous but rewarding; the view was said to be inspiring. I told her I preferred the view from the window. Perhaps the couple next door would go to breakfast soon and we could have the bed to ourselves.

"Think how invigorating a walk would be," she coaxed.

"I don't mind taking a walk," I told her, "but I'm not in the mood for hours of mountain climbing."

"It's not climbing," she insisted. "It's hiking."

"It's windy and cold up there," I pleaded, trying to woo her back under the covers.

I'm usually too eager to make love in the morning, while Norma prefers to wait — as if the day itself needed to embrace her first, whisper something special; as if morning were some kind of fore-play, to be savored like a kiss. Is it this way for most men and women? Some great but subtle difference breathed into us at birth? Perhaps women understand something men don't. Perhaps men hurry for a reason. Consider the ovum, bearer of generations, wait-ing serenely, confident of the future — while millions of sperm, tails whipping furiously, rush headlong toward their future.

"Bring a sweater and gloves," she said, disentangling herself from my embrace.

By the time we reached the foot of the trail, I'd stopped pout-ing. The day was chilly but sunny, the sky extravagantly blue. Sharp Top towered over us like a mountain in a dream, brooding and mysterious. A Park Service sign advised it would take an hour and a half to hike to the summit.

"They're exaggerating," I said to Norma. "It won't take that long." She turned toward me, a hint of amusement on her face, probably wondering whether I was challenging her, or the mountain, or was merely in a hurry to get back to bed. Mostly, I wanted to make the climb more interesting. To test our stamina, to go toe-to-toe against nature, against gravity, appealed to me. I like physical challenges; they're so unambiguous, so refreshingly straightforward — a wel-come relief from the dilemmas I face each day.

Taking the lead, Norma obliged by setting a vigorous pace — a little too vigorous, I thought. As we walked, she pointed to trees and rocks and fungi, to wild herbs and unusual plants. Norma never tires of explaining the natural world to me, telling me names we both know I promptly forget. Regrettably, I either ignore nature altogether or, a tad too rhapsodically, praise its great beauty. Like a hungry man, oblivious to subtleties of taste or fragrance, I wolf down the meal, compliments to the chef. I used to blame my ignorance of the natural world on growing up in the city, but the truth is I just don't pay enough attention; I'm too busy thinking about myself. Sometimes, Norma will plant something in our yard and wait, God knows how long, for me to notice. What I notice, staring out the window, is the changing weather of my emotions.

This day was no different. As Norma described the world around us, I meandered through the one inside my head. As nature jabbered away, birds cooing and leaves rustling, all I heard was my own voice, wheezing and nagging. Old scold, following me up the mountain, climbing me like a vine.

For nearly two years — ever since I'd stopped writing regularly for *The Sun* — I'd been beset by a haunting sense of failure. I worried that as a writer my best work, like some lengthening shadow, stretched behind me. Not only did I seem to have less time to write, I felt less driven, less willing to make the time.

I used to write an essay every month. It allowed me to define myself, declare myself, keep faith with the readers. The challenge wasn't merely to write honestly and artfully about my life; it was to wrest from a busy life the time to write, the countless hours I needed to craft decent sentences and point them toward the door. I'd stay up late to read manuscripts and answer mail and edit and proofread the upcoming issue, then get up at four in the morning to work on my essay. No matter how sleepy I was, no matter how broke or brokenhearted, I met my deadline. It was an act of will that strengthened me.

Yet if getting out an issue allowed me to feel like a hero, the writing itself was more problematic. I'd never learned to enjoy writing, to trust the roughness of a rough draft, to trust myself. I felt cursed with an intellect that seemed inadequate to the task — like a carpenter trying to build a house with a child's hammer and saw. Some mornings I couldn't even stand my own handwriting. My clumsy words sprawled in front of me. Get up, I'd tell them — and they'd hoot, as if I were nuts.

I'd rewrite the same sentence again and again, condemning my wordy imprecision, striving always for a kind of stylistic elegance that, even if I occasionally achieved it, hardly seemed genuine. Each piece was a struggle between the editor — who insisted on the polished phrase, the line that would live forever — and the writer, an ordinary man with something ordinary to say, something sentimental and unremarkable, not quite good enough.

Still, I mourned the absence of my voice in the magazine. Difficult as those essays were, they seemed worth the effort — especially when I'd hear that a particular line had touched someone, or that my openness about an embarrassing subject had moved readers to a greater honesty of their own.

Norma and I passed a creek curving down a staircase of fallen limbs and moss-covered rocks, and stopped for a moment. She asked what I was thinking and I told her, though she'd heard it all before.

"Stop blaming yourself," Norma said.

I looked at her and shrugged. "Who else am I going to blame?"

"That's not the point," she said. The point was to forgive myself for being unable to keep up the grinding pace of running a magazine and being a writer; for trying to make up for too little sleep with too much coffee; for shoving time out of the way month after month, year after year, and finally getting shoved back. Or had I forgotten the chest pains and the shortness of breath?

No, I hadn't forgotten. The doctor assured me there was nothing wrong with me, nothing physical. It was simply my body reacting to "stress." "Well, what am I supposed to do?" I asked him. Stress was as basic to my life as — well, breathing. Was he suggesting my *life* was the problem? "You could put it that way," he agreed.

I'd never worried about stress. The saints, the rebels, the dreamers of fugitive dreams — weren't their lives filled with stress? I was suspicious of people who seemed too relaxed. I objected to their slander of other people — people like me — as workaholics, as if being passionately engaged by life, being committed to something beyond security or pleasure, were some kind of pathology; as if sacrifice itself were ignoble. Wasn't there a difference between working hard for an ideal and working hard just to get ahead? But to my body it didn't seem to matter whether my allegiance was to a deadline or a bottom line.

Being unable to breathe forced me to look at my need to be a hero — which is the wrong line of questioning for a hero, if he wants to stay one. Was I writing because I had something important to say — or to prove to myself how important I was? Had my faith in words turned into some weird kind of religion, held together by the punishing ritual of the deadline?

Then, too, I worried that my essays were becoming too melancholy, too predictable. No matter what my subject, my writing really seemed to be about loss and incompletion, and about the travail of being me. Acknowledging the pain of living was one thing; exalting it was something else. I didn't want to be a poet of melancholy half-truths, preoccupied with my own little triumphs and disasters — and by the unremitting challenge of finding the right words for them. There was enough sadness in the world without my weeping. And there was more joy, more laughter, more wordless astonishment than my writing acknowledged.

I wondered if my dour view wasn't shaped in part by the way I wrote; by the looming menace of the deadline; by the oppressive editor in me who scowled at every line I put down. What would it mean, I asked, not to try to define and redeem myself in every issue, not to make everything I touched glow with the force of my will? What would it mean to sink into everything I *didn't* understand and *couldn't* put into words?

In the months that followed, I tried to write differently. I stopped writing monthly essays, to get away from a deadline. I tried to be more spontaneous, to separate the writer from the editor, the lightning flash of inspiration from the thunder of judgment. Try separating Siamese twins. Even the effort felt absurd, the worst kind of spiritual ambition, like trying to escape from myself, vault over the walls of my mind. Stuck with my old habits, I didn't become a better writer, just a slower one. Now, not having to finish a piece, I'd allow myself even more time to agonize over it. Freedom from a deadline turned out to be freedom to brood; to poke and pry at every word.

I wanted the writing to be more thoughtful, but it refused to be more thoughtful than *I* was. I wanted it to be better crafted, but the shape of the words was the shape I was in.

Which, I thought ruefully, wasn't as good as I'd imagined, as I struggled to keep up with Norma. The trail had become steeper, winding past low trees and tall, dry grasses. Here and there were patches of snow. I tried to gauge how far there was to go, but rock outcroppings blocked the view. I couldn't tell whether we were nearing the peak or merely coming to a change of grade.

We paused to catch our breath. Gazing down at the valley below us — at the forested slopes and grassy meadows, at the radiant face of the world, scrubbed and shiny — I felt bereft, as if staring into an abyss. Life without a deadline, I told Norma, was like splitting up with a lover — a passionate, selfish lover. You'd fought all the time. You knew you were better off without her. But now that she was gone you missed her, terribly.

Being forced to finish an essay, I said, challenged me like nothing else. Pushed to go deep, I went deeper — slipping past sleep's rusty gate, trespassing where I didn't belong. Invariably I was led to some discovery, some surprising encounter with myself. On the best nights, truth bowed to greet me; language opened her arms and told me I was home.

"The only thing worse than writing for a deadline is *not* writing for one," I sighed, loathing the sound of my voice. I'd never looked kindly on writers who whined about writing. As a friend put it, "Writers are among the luckiest of the lucky, and they know it. Writing isn't hard; digging ditches is hard." If I had never been comfortable calling myself a writer, I was at least someone who wrote; now, months went by without a word of mine in the magazine, and hardly a day without a lament.

As we went higher, the air grew colder, the wind more blustery. We were still hiking, not climbing, but to my aching calves the distinction was moot. When the narrow trail seemed to disappear altogether, we clambered over huge rocks on hands and knees. All my attention was focused now on moving upward, from rock to rock, ledge to ledge. Weary of talking, weary of thinking, I squinted against the harsh light, trying again to gauge how far there was to go.

What a relief at last to glimpse, looming ahead of us, Sharp Top's craggy peak. Miraculously shedding my fatigue, I bounded up the final rise. "What did I tell you?" I exulted. "Forty-five minutes! Half the time they said!"

The summit was spectacular. Big boulders jutted up like stone relics, ancient and ageless. Beneath us, visible for miles in every direction, was a patchwork of woods and fields and mossy green hills; farms with their barns and clustered outbuildings; roads leading to nearby towns; the motel far below and the silvery lake beside it, like a gleaming coin dropped from a great height.

We stood there, silently taking in the view. Luminous in the dazzling light, the valley was, unarguably, beautiful. Yet I didn't find it that inspiring. Admittedly, I wasn't having a great day, but it seemed a bit too perfect, too pretty, nature in its Sunday best. I wondered what this land looked like long ago. Before motels and man-made lakes. Before the settlers conquered the wilderness — felling trees, driving plows across the land. I wondered about the Native Americans who journeyed here regularly for thousands of years. How could Sharp Top's lonely, wind-swept heights not have beckoned to them? I didn't know much about vision quests or shamanic practices, but it seemed likely this had been some sort of holy ground, perhaps a place of testing and initiation, of sacred rituals.

Native Americans, I suspected, regarded the land in a way that was hard for me to conceive, shaping themselves to it instead of the other way around. Wendell Berry once observed that the pristine America seen by the first white men can't even be imagined anymore; it's a lost continent, sunk like Atlantis in the sea. As a culture, I mused, we're estranged from the land because we live by imposing ourselves on it. Not unlike, I thought wryly, my editor's hand, forever fussing and rearranging; I could no more leave a sentence alone than the settlers could leave this valley alone.

We spent the afternoon in bed — our passion a kind of solace. Though I hated to burden passion that way, I needed reminding that words aren't the only way to touch. Our neighbors weren't around — but just in case, we put on a jazz tape, and let it play over and over, a mournful oboe slipping in and out of the music like a thief.

When the sun went down, we dragged a couple of chairs outside, wrapped ourselves in a blanket, and watched the woods fill with shadows. I gazed up at Sharp Top, immense in the distance — and for a fleeting moment, I thought I was seeing it for the first time. How wild it looked, how ghostly and unfamiliar. I stared, lost in wonder. Slowly, the morning came back to me, like a remembered dream: this was the mountain I'd conquered. How odd that memory could betray me so profoundly. Or was it the gathering darkness that fooled me, some trick of the fading light?

I told Norma how remote Sharp Top seemed, as if we hadn't even been up there. We talked about our tendency to turn an experience into an accomplishment — as if life were a series of goals, of little triumphs stretching into the future. For a moment, at the summit, we ooh and aah at the view, plant our flag, watch it wave in the sad wind. But we don't stay long, so that life itself feels unlived, as remote as a distant mountain.

"Well," Norma said, "why don't we hike it again tomorrow?" I laughed, but she was serious. "We could take our time," she insisted.

I reminded her we needed to leave early. "Besides," I said, "I'd rather be left with this sense of poignancy."

"Better," she said, "to be left with a different memory."

We sat there, not saying much as the sky grew darker and the first stars came out. A fat moon rose over the horizon, casting the mountain in an even eerier light. Perhaps Sharp Top would have seemed mysterious no matter how patiently, how attentively, we had hiked it; perhaps there was some mystery we weren't meant to take down with us. But when I thought about the dark crags and barren slopes and the giant boulders at the summit — when I thought about standing breathless beside the lonely beauty of those big rocks, proud of having reached them in forty-five minutes, a big grin on my face — I was ashamed.

It's one thing, I thought, to wring my hands about civilization, and the greed of those who ravage the planet, yet isn't ignoring nature a way of dominating it, too? How little I knew, I reflected sadly, about the spirit of dead Native Americans or the living spirit of a mountain. I felt a sudden longing for something I couldn't name, some lost communion with the world, with myself.

Dry leaves scurried by, lifted by the wind. All the conflicts that ever haunted me as a writer haunted me still; I felt as far from the sacredness of words as a shopping mall was from the sacredness of the land. Would I ever change? Would I give up imagining I needed to conquer myself, scale the heights? I didn't know. I wanted to be a real writer, not a parody of one. Yet I didn't trust my thoughts and feelings. No wonder my pieces had at their heart such loneliness, reaching through the words but afraid to reach too far, be too raw. The dream of turning writing into something joyous and fulfilling seemed as unattainable as ever — each essay a mountain to climb, a forced march to the end.

This Body

MY DAUGHTERS want to know why I've started working out at the Y. I want bigger muscles, I tell them. I want to be stronger. They think this is hilarious: a forty-six-year-old man acting like he's sixteen.

But at sixteen, I acted forty-six. I began college that year and was too busy for sports, too serious. A couple of decades later, I took up running, which is terrific for endurance but does nothing for my flabby middle, my shoulders, my arms, my chest.

My daughters still don't get it. To them, my body is familiar, predictable, a fixed star in the firmament of middle age. It's a father's body, sour with the sweats of work and worry, strong enough.

What difference does it make how I look? Instead of straining to do one more overhead press, I could be at the Columbia Street Bakery, drinking coffee and reading the newspaper. I could be nibbling on a bran muffin or — life is short — a raspberry-chocolate croissant, instead of getting right up in gravity's face, adding ten more pounds to the bar.

The eight Nautilus machines face a wall-to-wall mirror in a windowless room. With their creaking cams and chains, they look like they belong in a medieval dungeon. In this more secular age, we torture ourselves.

My interrogator eyes me coolly. *I won't deny it,* I say. *I'm goaded by vanity. I tried to love my body — all those years of psychotherapy — but it was like trying to love spinach.* He lights a cigarette. *I figured maybe I'd love myself more if I looked better.* He raises an eyebrow. *OK, I admit, that's not real love.* He nods. *But it feels great: the body called from slumber, a troubled dream of irrelevance, fat replaced by muscle, arms and chest taking on a more defined shape.* Very good, he says. Two more sets, he says. And remember, you don't build strength by repeating easy movements. Once you can overcome the resistance, you must increase it. When you work at the limit of your strength, you force the muscle to adapt.

This is a metaphor for life, I think. What's that line from Rilke? *The purpose of life is to be defeated by greater and greater things.* But

I spend enough time thinking. I'm here to work the lower back and the abdominals, not to think. I'm here to do the duo squat, the leg curl, the pullover, the arm cross, the decline press, the lateral raise, the overhead press, the arm extension, the arm curl. I'm here because my ancestors were large, heavily muscled animals, who for millions of years ran down other animals for food, while I sit at a desk all day, running down fleeting thoughts. I'm here because I'm estranged from my body, rarely knowing myself through dint of hard work. I'm here because when I was a kid, I asked for a set of weights and got a lecture instead about how weight lifters are muscle-bound, not to mention stupid and conceited. Was my father threatened, worried that I might become stronger than he?

Cut the crap, my interrogator warns. *You're here because you're a privileged white male who can afford to work out instead of work. You're here, spending too much time resting between sets, while real men — and real women, too — are getting out of bed, groggily getting dressed, and shuffling off to a day of real work.*

The people here are real enough for me. There's the burly truck driver who boasts, not long after the Gulf War, that his son has joined the Air Force. There's the house painter who chides me when I change the dial from the rock station to National Public Radio. There's the Vietnam vet who scolds me for not breathing right: exhale during the pressing part of the lift, he warns, inhale on the return. Momentarily confused, I stop breathing altogether. He shakes his head. And don't forget to breathe, he sighs.

But we don't talk much. I'm here to exercise my body, not my big mouth. I'm here to stop being bullied by the past, to stop making excuses, to stop pretending on hot summer days that it's not really hot enough to strip off my shirt.

Of course, there are mornings I don't show up at all, when I'm too busy or too depressed, when I don't want to look like another middle-aged man trying to stop the inevitable ruin of his body. Time has already taken a couple of bites; it likes the taste. But the next morning I'm back, winking in the mirror at the fool who's determined to be lean, tough, and chewy before time licks the plate.

GRADUATION

IT WAS A PERFECT DAY, the sky clear, as blue and true as a pledge of love. On the campus, the magnolias were in bloom, the huge, creamy white flowers richly fragrant. Spring was everywhere, shamelessly beautiful, wet lips laughing, hair unpinned.

I wanted it, like all perfect days, to last, though I knew it would last only in memory. There it might endure, as a celebration and a passage, a graduation day. For Norma, it meant she was now a doctor — in the eyes of the world, if not yet in her own. For us, it meant we had survived the rigors that medical school imposes on a marriage; we, too, had passed a test.

I wanted the day to last, as I wanted *us* to last: our pleasures; our worries; who we were now, never to be again, shaped by this moment, this unforgettable moment, which of course we would one day forget. I wanted to remember how rich these years had been, and how arid; the nights she wasn't home; the bright moonlight on the empty bed.

I hadn't wanted Norma to go to medical school. I argued fervently against the medical establishment; against science, great voodoo religion of the West; against the misplaced notion that people are reducible to their parts, instead of whole, flesh and soul.

But the real reason I didn't want her to go was that I didn't want her to go. Away. From me. I didn't want medical school to be more important to her than I was, more important than my irreducible soul. I wanted a wife I could turn to. I wanted shelter from the dark skies of worry and the days when everything went wrong. I didn't want her to study all night. I wanted her beside me, where I could study her. I wanted to ask my question, and hear her breathless answer, and ask it a little differently, and hear her answer again. I wanted a shared life, not separate rooms in the house of ambition. I wanted her to believe not in a career but in our enduring bond. I wanted her to be my refuge, I wanted to be her comfort.

Oh fear, blowing a kiss and calling it love.

I looked to Norma as to a sky of endless promise, the way a prisoner gazes yearningly from the window in his cell. Was it Norma

I wanted, or freedom from my loneliness? Was it medical school I feared, or my own unruly self?

Her first two years were spent in classrooms and in labs — and in front of textbooks each night. Histology. Physiology. Pharmacology. Embryology. The names meant little to me, like towns you pass on a train, stations that sit in the dark of the mind, foreign and strange. Norma would tell me stories about these places, in words she knew I could understand, in words even a ten-year-old could understand. Yet I rarely responded with excitement, or invited her to tell me more. I *wanted* to care about the intricacies of cells, the mysteries of tissue and organ and bone, but what I *really* cared about was when she would be done studying. Or whether she'd be home in time for dinner. Or how she could get that terrible smell out of her hair.

First-year students are given a human cadaver to dissect, the cold, gray body preserved in formaldehyde. For eight months, with scalpel and scissors and sometimes with just her hands, Norma laid back the veins, the arteries, the muscle, the fat, feeling into the inward parts, the secret rooms that once pulsed with a ruby glow, now revealed to curious eyes. For eight months, she labored in that not-so-final, not-so-resting place for souls who lingered ghostly — who can doubt it? — while their bodies were treated thus. For eight months, in that drab, gray room that reeked of formaldehyde and death and nervous sweat, she labored in the heat and the stink, cutting and memorizing, cutting and cutting at the tough, cord-like muscles, at the bony skull that had to be sectioned with a hacksaw so she could get to the brain, cutting through the haze of death and mystery and ignorance, and through the haze of formaldehyde that clung to everything, to the cold, steel tables and the cold, gray bodies, and to her, no matter how much she scrubbed. So that at night, faint but unmistakable, that ghastly smell lingered. For eight months. In my lovely wife's long, dark hair.

What bothered Norma most of all, she told me one night, was dissecting the hands. They seemed to her the most intimate part of the man, so that in touching his hands, she was touching what he had touched, was touching *him*, his life suddenly real to her.

As she told me this, she held my hand, her touch astonishingly tender. She held me the way you wish you'd held someone when you still had the chance, held the woman or the man, the father or the mother, the daughter or the son, held them in awe, held them for a luminous moment in which grief and joy, death and life, are one. How we long for such a touch! How we ache to be known! Each of us will die, yet this we deny, and thus deny each other. And so we do not touch, but play lightly with each other; or squeeze each other, meat to meat; or clutch each other, so our longing itself will disguise our need, so the long cry of the body cries out instead, *I love you, kiss me, kiss me again.*

Two years of facts, endless facts: facts about this and facts about that, illuminating parts but not the whole, while patients go on dying, despite the facts, or recover miraculously, despite the facts; facts that show why people suffer, but ignore insufferably who they are — how they live and where they work and why they suffer their broken hearts. Two years of lectures and textbooks and facts, and Norma was ready for the wards.

That's how they train our doctors. For two years, they fill their heads with scientific knowledge that seems to explain so much. Then they send them out, with their white coats, with their knowledge. They send them into the dizzying complexity of a modern hospital, into the wards, to see real people, not textbook cases: the man clutching his chest, crying without shame and without hope; the woman moaning through early labor; the child lying listlessly in her bed, the sheets too tidy, too neatly tucked in, not a child's bed at all but a bed a child will die in. Here, amidst the corridors that seem to stretch endlessly; here, where you can get lost looking for a room, or an answer; here, the curriculum changes.

In her white coat, with her stethoscope, Norma was virtually indistinguishable from the rest of the staff — the interns and residents and attending physicians. Every few months, she rotated through a different service — surgery, internal medicine, obstetrics and gynecology, psychiatry, family practice — each a separate world, with its own rules and customs, passions and politics.

There was the surgeon from Texas, who insisted that country-and-western music be piped into the operating room. There were doctors who treated diseases rather than people; those who put money first; those who made mistakes and tried to hide them. And doctors who were sincere and caring, who still believed in talking with patients and in small, redeeming acts of mercy. The best of them knew that no matter how strong the medicine, healing is always affected by more than the intended cure; that we are affected by everything — what we eat, the weather, our dreams, our relationships, our faith or lack of it. These doctors knew how to listen to their patients, and to their own hearts. They honored the shimmering mystery we are — even as pain knots our insides, and our life leaks away. One doctor, asked by a student how he kept from being overwhelmed by all the suffering, answered: have you ever been in a great cathedral? Yes, the student said. What did it feel like? The student remembered the awe, the reverence, the sense of being in the presence of something greater than herself. The doctor nodded.

But such an attitude was rare. The real reverence seemed to be reserved for machines — for the CT scanners and computers and diagnostic devices that have so transformed medicine and increasingly taken the place of a physician's intuition and common sense. How impressive these machines; they do, after all, save lives. But in the service of a growing medical technology, how much of our lives is denied? What about the personal and social ills that don't fit into the diagnostic categories? What about the radically different ways of understanding and healing ourselves, which the technicians reject? Prayer. Meditation. Herbs. Acupuncture. Diet. Yoga. Tai Chi. Massage. The data isn't in, they say.

Yet the data *is* in on conventional medicine, and it's hardly reassuring. How much they don't know, these doctors rushing down the hall with their white coats and their clipboards and their harried commands. They're on their way to a "code," rushing to save someone's life. They're good at this — at descending like a flock of snow-white birds on a tired old man whose heart has given out, at shocking the old heart back to life. Maybe tomorrow they'll give him a new heart or new kidneys or a new liver. It's become easier to replace broken parts than to explain why they're broken; easier to condemn unorthodox remedies than to acknowledge medicine's failure to deal with cancer or Alzheimer's or multiple sclerosis or rheumatoid arthritis or stroke or AIDS.

Even when the doctors don't have a clue what to do, when they're as lost as children in a driving rain, they still do something. More tests are ordered; another operation is scheduled; one more piece of expensive equipment is wheeled in. In the face of human suffering — and in the face of their own ignorance — the hardest thing for doctors to do is nothing. That's one reason hospitals are such busy places, such busy and expensive places. That's one reason a medical education is so grueling, demanding of third- and fourth-year students sixty, seventy, eighty hours a week.

It's an initiation of the crudest kind, like boot camp, or hazing: the broken sleep; the exhaustion; the worry about doing something wrong. Their lives slip away from them, like the words of a half-forgotten song. Working all day, then all night, they drift through the corridors of sleeplessness, on call for thirty-six hours at a time, wanting nothing more than to lie down in a cool, dark place and sleep, or weep. They become doctors by learning to deny themselves: their sleepiness; the slow length of their feelings; their quiet, dreamy knowing; the secret knowledge inside. The corridors lead them into the sunken kingdom of certainty, of technological wizardry, of drugs that plunge the body into war with itself, pounding it into a stupor with chemical fists. Yet all the while, they ignore what health really is.

Norma didn't want to be that kind of doctor. Trained as a dancer, she still moved like one, with a lightness that rose from her like mist. Whenever she had time, she exercised; she ran; she ate well-balanced meals. For years she'd taught natural-foods cooking. To her, health wasn't just the absence of disease, but a measure of our wholeness: mind and body, dark clouds and green fields. Intuitively faithful to nature's cycles, Norma was happiest when outdoors — walking in the woods or gardening. Regrettably, being a student didn't leave much time for this.

Nearly thirty when she entered medical school — a mother, in her second marriage — she was older than many of her classmates, and even some of her teachers. This gave her an edge in maturity, but meant she had to endure the startling arrogance of doctors who were younger than she, and who acted it. (One morning, the chief resident was leading rounds, interns and students trailing behind him. His mind was on last night's game: the first half, the second half, the stunning rebound, the spectacular pass. He couldn't stop talking to the doctor beside him about the amazing grace and self-assurance of the Carolina players, the way that final shot arched into the air. Students described this patient's progress, that patient's symptoms, the bland and boring roster of human aches and pains. Unaware, uncaring, the chief resident kept talking. Until Norma exploded, like Carolina in the last seconds of play. *Shut up*, she snapped. Students don't talk that way to chief residents, but the point was hers.)

For the most part, Norma endured silently the bad manners, the bad food, the fluorescent din. She endured the hodgepodge of fact and superstition — her scientific mind thrilled by medicine's scientific rigor, her common sense agape at everything science omits. She endured the long hours, the lack of sleep, the fading light of the days she never got to see. But worst of all — worse than the seasons that kept changing without her, worse than new life springing up without her — was coming home to the man she loved, to his odd, unfathomable grief.

Norma knew how the past can pull at you, like the moon pulls at your heart. She knew how abandoned I'd felt as a child, how I feared being abandoned again. Knowing this, she still couldn't fathom my sadness. Fathom the rain, collecting in black puddles at your feet. Fathom the wild lament in a man, the loneliness in his being.

Neither could she bear being blamed for it. After she'd spent a day and a night at the hospital, looking at hideously deformed infants, at backs eaten away by bedsores, my accusing gaze was the last thing she wanted to see. It didn't make it any easier that she also blamed herself. Part of her wanted to be the dutiful wife, the kind of wife her mother had taught her to be, who would make the rooms of my life a home. The voices of the past, the sighing hearth, called to her, but the future led somewhere else. She knew the road she had to follow; it meant leaving behind the part of her that would have sacrificed herself for my sorrows.

You might think I knew better than to ask. You might think I'd learned not to treat a woman as a sex object, or a love object. Then again, you might think I'd learned nothing — that, in my third marriage, I was as big a fool as when I first tried to kiss a girl and missed, my lips aimed at hers but grazing her nose instead and landing wetly on her cheek. What was it Ray Bradbury said? The first thing you learn in life is that you're a fool; the last thing you learn is that you're the same fool.

I grew up worshiping a jealous god, a tell-me-you-love-me god. A sacrifice was exactly what he wanted. Prepare a place for her, he said, at the towering altar; make her stay with you, until the long night is over. The idea that Norma owed me nothing — that the sweet, secret center of her life was hers alone — was blasphemy to this god, who knew a woman's place was in the home.

It's hard to turn your back on a god like this. Yet this was my curriculum: to let go of what I imagined was my security; to trust that whether or not Norma was beside me, our bond would endure.

It wasn't easy. Our heavens and hells, for being self-created, seem no less real. Fear of abandonment is a pale phrase, as gray and lifeless as a cadaver. But whether or not I acknowledge it, the past is with me, closer than the closest friend. I am the sum of my experience, a body of experience — some of it joyous, some sad.

Why did I love being alone in the morning, cherishing the solitude and the stillness, and hate being alone at night? Why, when I most needed them, was I reluctant to reach out to friends? Why, when I most needed it, was I unable to comfort myself?

My loneliness was like a letter I carried with me, and glanced at nervously, and folded and unfolded, but never read; a letter I gave instead to every woman who ever loved me, as if this clue to my longing were addressed to her, as if I didn't recognize, in the rise and fall of the writing, my own boyish hand.

The child in me needed my love as much as I needed Norma's; needed me to pay attention to him after all these years. It was my presence he wanted, not Norma's sacrifice; my kindness, not the embers of someone else's dream. Because Norma was away so much — because I had no choice, really — I started to befriend him. Perhaps the only time we grow is when we have no choice; when life blows down the door before we can say "come in." If, because of Norma's absence, I learned to love myself a little more, shall I say that I'm sorry or grateful, that these years were a burden or a gift?

At the graduation, cameras were everywhere, as proud families tried to capture the fleeting essence of the day. Capped and gowned graduates, doctors now, were being posed by eager parents as though they were still kids. Everyone, it seemed, was being lined up for a photograph or taking one, smiling for the camera or fiddling with one. How godlike the camera, which seems to capture and pre-serve the moment — preserve it for that one day in the future when we want to hold in our hands the past.

I, too, had a camera, yet I doubted I would capture much of anything. Not the fleeting essence, that's for sure. You take a pho-tograph, imagining you've captured the moment; but when you reach for it, it's not there. There's just you, reaching. Photographs don't lie, but we do — about everything that's left out of the frame.

I have a photograph of Norma accepting her diploma. I have another, taken a moment later, of her walking across the stage. I have a picture of her parents, beaming — at this grown woman, a doctor now, their little girl, oldest of eight.

I have another picture, which someone else took. Norma and I are laughing, but I can't remember why. The moment is gone, like the four years that came before it, the laughter softening and for-giving the faces in the frame.

LEGACY

T HE MAN'S VOICE was rich and confident — he sounded
like someone accustomed to speaking with authority — but there
was worry in it, some sadness running like a quiet creek alongside
his words.

He was calling to talk about his son, who had been arrested on
drug charges, found guilty, and sentenced to eighteen months. He
feared for his son's safety. Harassed by other prisoners, as well as by
guards, his son was vulnerable, and the father knew it. "He's just a
middle-class kid," he said, aware that the same credentials that get
you into college or a country club may make life more difficult
behind bars, among blacks and Hispanics hostile to whites, to privi-
lege.

The father had done what he could to get his son a lighter sentence. Now, he was trying to get him transferred. Thus far
unsuccessful, he continued petitioning friends, politicians. Every
weekend, he made the two-thousand-mile round trip to visit. At
least, he said, he could help his son do his time.

I understood his feelings. A parent myself, I knew that innermost longing in me for my children's well-being; the fierce instinct
to protect them from harm, unequivocal as the elk's flared nostrils
and lowered horns at the warning rustle in the grass. The need to
protect and guide one's children changes over time. This is their
world, too, with its lessons to teach; to stand in the way would be
foolish. Yet the yearning persists. "You're never done being a parent," he said.

His call touched me, and not just because I'm a parent. It reminded me of my own parents, and my unending bond with them.
No matter if your parents are close or distant, no matter if the
bond seems withered, like an old vine wrapped around a dead
branch, it's still a bond. Friends and lovers and wives have come
and gone. I'm changed and unchanging: still a son.

When I was younger, I naively imagined that by leaving home I
could leave behind my conflicts with my parents, only to discover

they would mysteriously resurface in other relationships. Eventually, I began to understand how much of my emotional life was shaped by feelings long suppressed, stored for years in the dark folds of memory and in a body armored against itself.

We were all wounded in some way by our parents, not because they were evil, or wished us harm, but because they too were wounded, like their parents before them. Who among us, born needing to be loved, did not soon learn our parents couldn't love us for who we were? They needed us to smile, to coo, to be quiet, to succeed, perhaps not to succeed. They needed us to conspire with them to deny their scars.

Nearly twenty years ago, I understood for the first time that I'd been performing all my life for my father. Bent over my typewriter, in my lonely room thousands of miles from home, I was still on stage, and the only applause that mattered was his. I stopped writing for six months, while I considered whether I wrote out of a deep necessity to express certain ideas, or merely out of a necessity to be a writer. I've been writing all my adult life and, still, that distinction isn't clear. I struggle with what it means to be a writer and what it means to be my father's son, trying to understand the extent of my allegiance to his ideals and his confusions, his hatreds and his loves. He's been dead thirteen years, but he's with me when I sit down at the typewriter and lie down with my wife; in the comforts I've made mine; in the vows I've made and in the vows I've broken. "You have to dig deep to bury your daddy," the gypsies say.

My father was a salesman — what Arthur Miller called "a man out there in the blue riding on a smile and a shoeshine" — and was sometimes successful, sometimes not. Our family fortunes rose and fell on the high seas of his imagination: he had more implausible ideas for getting rich, and less aptitude for making them work, than most men. Often, when I was a child, he'd sadly tell me how much he had wanted to leave me a "legacy," but had failed. There was no money, no property. I'd tell him that wasn't important, that he wasn't a failure, that the only riches I wanted were his friendship, his presence, his time. My assurances were utterly sincere but unconvincing. How was I to know, as a boy, how shoddy a piece of merchandise his life was to him? How could I mourn with him his business failures or his failures at love or his failure to succeed, in the years before I was born, at one of the few things that had really mattered to him?

Before he became a salesman, he had wanted to sell words: his own. He had wanted to be a writer. I can't say why he didn't succeed — whether he couldn't make enough money or wasn't good enough. I can't say how hard he tried. He called himself a "frustrated writer," but did that mean his writing was never recognized — or that he had neither the time nor the patience nor the courage to write?

He found the time to read what I wrote — to read, to criticize, to edit, sometimes to rewrite completely what I'd done. You could say my writing got more attention than I did. If, at times, I welcomed his help, I also knew it was help I couldn't refuse, advice I wasn't free to challenge. Because of him, my writing improved — my book reports and essays nearly always earned A's — but it turned into something that was no longer mine.

Nothing has a stronger influence on us psychologically, Jung said, than the "unlived life" of our parents. My father never told me he wanted me to be a writer; he didn't have to. Even in a family as given as ours to endless discussion, and endless complaining, the really important feelings were rarely put into words.

After all these years, I still can't say how much my need to write has to do with my innermost sense of purpose and how much has to do with him. Following the clues is like making my way down a hallway in darkness. These sentences, which seem to move across the page so surely, trail ghosts behind them. Are the words really mine? When I tell myself the words aren't good enough — which is my harsh judgment about nearly everything I write — is that my voice, or his?

My father was inordinately proud of my accomplishments as the editor of my high-school and college papers and, later, as a journalist in New York; he carried in his wallet my yellowing clips; he boasted to his friends of my awards. But he never gave up imagining he had something to teach me. In nearly everything I wrote, he found fault. He didn't understand the difference between wanting me to be good and demanding it, his love for me burdened by the grief he denied in himself.

Not all my memories of him are painful. There was tenderness between us, and humor, and a kind of camaraderie I've never known with anyone else. He was my father. I drank up who he was like a parched root drinks the rain — his love, his misery, his ambitions, his failures. For better and worse, he shaped me, and gambled on me to redeem him. For better and worse, my words give a shape to what was unredeemed and unexpressed in him.

The cover and text of *Four In The Morning* were designed by Sue Koenigshofer of SCK Design.

The cover is composed of photographs by Will May, George Peer, and Barbara Tyroler. They were combined and tinted on computer by Marvin Forte of Chapel Hill Printing. The photograph of the author is by John Rosenthal. Imagesetting was done by Kathy Goforth and Claire Gingell at Colonial Press. The book was printed on 55-pound Huron Natural recycled paper by Thomson-Shore in Dexter, Michigan.

The text was set in a typeface known as Garamond, designed by Claude Garamond and adapted for the computer by Adobe in 1989 — some four hundred years too late for Claude, who died in poverty in Paris. The titles are set in Palatino Bold, designed by a sixteenth-century Italian calligrapher named Giovanni Palatino.

The essays were written in the twentieth century, in North Carolina, in the hours before dawn.